I0524628

THE BLACK IRON EMPIRE

THE SOUL BOUND SAGA
BOOK FOUR

JAMES E WISHER

SAND HILL PUBLISHING

Edited by: Janie Linn Dullard

Cover art by: B-Ro

ISBN: 978-1-68520-035-0

010120231.0

CHAPTER 1

J oran stood, hunched over against the wind, atop one of the jutting columns that formed a sort of path between the island where they arrived and the next closest one to the north. Black clouds blotted out the sun, making midmorning feel more like twilight. Thunder cracked and lightning ran through the clouds without arcing to the ground. So far at least, the sky had only threatened to kill them, it hadn't actually tried. He dearly hoped to be off of these far-too-small pillars when it did.

His soulmate, Mia, stood in front of him preparing herself to jump to the next pillar. She had her silver sword belted at her waist and a look of grim determination on her face. The wind ruffled her short, black hair, but otherwise didn't seem to faze her.

The dwarves, Grub and Stoneheart, stayed behind him alternating between aloof indifference and glares of hatred, most of the latter coming from Stoneheart. It seemed nothing would convince the centurion that Grub truly held the empire's best interests at heart. Joran had told them both more than once that, given their current situation, fighting amongst themselves would only make matters worse.

He felt certain they believed him regardless of their sullen behavior. At least they hadn't gotten into any further shouting matches. Of course, the fact that the wind made it nearly impossible to hear anything may have had something to do with the lack of arguing as well. He didn't actually care as long as they did nothing that lessened their odds of reaching the second island.

"Are you ready?" Mia asked. Her words barely reached him over the howls of the wind.

Joran nodded, not wanting to yell himself hoarse.

She gathered herself and leapt with supernatural grace to land easily on the next pillar in a maybe twenty-foot diameter landing zone. It seemed big, but the wind pushing you around made the landing difficult. Or at least more difficult than it seemed for her. Their soul bond had given Mia physical enhancements that made her one of the most dangerous fighters in the world. Joran got clarity of thought that helped him see the best course to take in almost any situation.

Useful, but right now he'd trade all the clarity of thought in the world for a little extra muscle in his thighs.

Mia waved at him to join her.

Right, here we go again.

As soon as the most recent gust passed, he took two strides and jumped with all his might.

His right foot hit the edge of the pillar.

Something crumbled.

His heart leapt into his throat, but Mia grabbed him and pulled him to safety. Joran fell to his knees gasping for breath. That had been the closest one so far.

"You good?" she asked.

"I'm alive, thanks to you. I'm also glad we don't have to do this too many more times."

"Think we'll find anything good on the next island?"

Joran forced himself to stand. "I don't know what we'll find, but if it's as dead as that last rock and we can't find anything to drink, well, I'm trying not to think about it."

"Think about it," Mia insisted. "You're good at thinking. If anyone can get us out of this mess, it's you."

Her faith heartened him even as he feared it might be misplaced. Unless they found food and water, he could think as hard as he wanted, but it wouldn't stop them from starving to death.

"I'll do my best."

They moved back to make room for Grub and Stoneheart. They glared at each other one last time before Stoneheart moved as far back as the pillar would allow, ran forward, and leapt. He made it more easily than Joran had despite his armor, a testament to the warrior's strength.

Grub took a slightly different path. Ether flowed into his legs and he sprang easily across. Joran needed to learn that spell. It seemed easy enough, but so far he hadn't dared risk it. With a week of practice and nothing on the line, maybe he'd give it a try, but certainly not now.

When everyone had caught their breath, they repeated the process over to the next pillar. Luckily for Joran, this one had a smaller gap and he made the jump without issue.

After what seemed like a long time but was probably no more than an hour, they all rested, safe and sound, on the new island. All of them save Mia breathed hard. For her part, she stayed a little ways apart from the group, hand on the hilt of her sword, ready for any danger that might appear.

Joran thanked any power that might be listening that he'd ended up with her as his soulmate.

When he'd finally caught his breath Joran asked, "Grub, can you use your magic to find us some water?"

The geomancer made a sour face. "I can try, but there's so

3

much corruption both in the earth and the air that I have no idea how the magic will work."

"I can see the darkness swirling in the ether, but I can't feel it. Can you?" Joran asked.

Grub and Stoneheart both stared at him as if he'd suddenly grown a second head.

"You can't feel the oppressive weight, Lord Den Cade?" Stoneheart asked.

Joran shook his head. "Mia, do you feel anything?"

She turned his way. "I feel nothing out of the ordinary. Certainly there's no oppressive weight trying to crush me."

Joran seriously doubted that corruption affected dwarves more than humans. If anything, he imagined it would be the opposite. That meant something else left them more vulnerable. But what?

"Grub, look at me, Mia, and Stoneheart through the ether and see if anything jumps out at you." Joran followed his own request and shifted his vision to the ether.

The dark threads of corruption ran all through the chaotic energy, just as it did every time he looked. Those threads pierced Grub and Stoneheart, but when he looked at Mia it appeared the threads couldn't get close to her. Some sort of glowing barrier stopped them. Since he knew Mia had no skill with magic, something else had to be causing the corruption to leave her alone.

His gaze took in every inch of her and finally he noticed her sword. Every time a black thread drifted into it, the thread vanished in a dark puff of corruption. It affected ethereal corruption the same way it had affected the black sword back in Tiber. Amazing, that made it even more useful than he'd first thought.

"There's a glow coming from your pocket," Grub said.

Joran pulled out the amulet he took from Samaritan. As soon as he had it out the disintegrating threads of corruption grew visible. So the amulet had the same power as Mia's sword. That suggested they had the same source, the Prophet.

As soon as the thought entered his head, he dismissed it. No way would the pope let a newly inducted White Knight anywhere near a holy relic.

Alright, if Samaritan didn't get it from the Prophet, then he must have succeeded in tracking the fraud back to wherever he came from and found the amulet there. That quest got him put on the church's hit list after all.

Interesting as he found that line of speculation, Joran set it aside for another time. "Take the amulet, Grub. Maybe having it will make your magic work better."

"No!" Mia put herself immediately between Joran and Grub. "You'll lose your protection without the amulet."

"Maybe, but I have a theory. As long as you have the silver sword, I may be protected through our link. I never felt the discomfort Stoneheart and Grub described even before you took the amulet from Samaritan. And, to be totally honest, if Grub can't find us water at least, we won't live long enough for my lack of protection to be an issue."

"I still don't like it." Mia moved aside and Joran handed the amulet to Grub. "Well?"

"I'm okay," Joran said. "There's a minor headache forming in the back of my skull, but other than that, I think I'm good."

She shot him a look that suggested she didn't fully believe him, but he wouldn't be able to lie to her with their link. She was probably just feeling overly protective.

Grub ignored them, eyes closed, as ether swirled around the amulet. Corrupt energy went in and pure ether came out. A remarkable and fascinating sight. Joran had no idea how it worked, but he would like to find out.

His headache grew quickly worse, so he released his view of the ether. The moment he did, the pain receded to a dull ache. It didn't take a genius to figure out that interacting with the corrupt ether had a negative effect on his health.

He resolved only to touch it in an emergency.

"I found… something," Grub said at last. "It feels like water, but polluted by corruption. I can't find anything pure."

"Then what good are you?" Stoneheart asked.

Grub glared at him. "I don't see you doing anything useful."

"Enough, both of you." The headache did nothing to help Joran's temper. "Stoneheart, not another derogatory word about Grub or so help me I'll see you busted down to stable hand when we get back. Grub, take point. Show us the water you found. Purifying it won't be an issue."

The two dwarves grumbled, but no further complaints were made. Good. Joran was thoroughly sick of listening to the pair bicker.

"How are you going to purify the water?" Mia asked as they set out behind Grub.

"I'm not." Joran patted her right hand, the one that held the silver sword's hilt. "You are."

Her eyes nearly popped out of her head. "I don't know how to do any of that magic stuff. All I know how to do is fight."

"You don't have to do any magic. Remember how the black sword reacted when you touched the silver sword to it? I suspect purification of the black sword's corruption caused it. Assuming we find water, all you need to do is put your sword into it and let it work. Nothing simpler."

She frowned. "Are you sure? That sounds too simple."

"I'm not sure of anything, but everything I've observed tells me that will work. If I'm wrong, we'll just have to think of something else to try. Success or death tends to focus the mind."

Grub led them away from the cliff face and across a blackened plain of dirt and jutting stones. The land looked exactly the same as the first island. Still no sign of animals or plants. He tried and failed to imagine what might have caused devastation on this scale. Even the giant serpent lacked the power to ruin the land so completely. Joran despaired of their chances to survive in such a hellish landscape.

He lost all track of time as they marched across the unchanging terrain. In the distance, some hills rose, their sides as black as the plain around them. From the looks of it, this island had to be much larger than the one where they started.

The only good thing about the wretched area was a lack of aggressive beasts or monsters. Not that the lack of life led Mia to relax. Every time he looked her way her gaze darted left and right as if she expected an attack at any moment.

"You seem rather antsy given the lack of anything dangerous around," Joran said. "Do you see something that I don't?"

Mia shook her head. "No, but this place gives me the creeps. It makes my skin crawl, and I usually only get that feeling when someone's watching me, usually with an arrow nocked and ready to loose."

Joran looked around again, even risking a glance into the ether just to make sure, but there simply wasn't anything to see. Whatever bothered Mia had to be in her imagination.

At least he hoped so.

CHAPTER 2

Bright sunlight shone down on Overseer and the thrashing, screaming mercenaries. Well, to be fair, they weren't actually screaming or thrashing. The paralyzing magic Overseer had used on them prevented them from moving or making a sound, but their fear and panic washed over him like psychic music and he knew the dance of pain they wanted to make intimately. Every demon in every hell knew that dance and loved it. At least, when the demon in question wasn't the one performing it. If the anticipation of being transformed did this to them, he couldn't wait to see what happened when he actually began the process.

He bound them with his magic only seconds after the archbishop sent him the Black Bile he needed to transform them into bile zombies. After weeks trudging beside the miserable creatures, he couldn't wait to kill them all and turn them into something useful. Shock quickly gave way to understanding which transformed into panic and fear, two of Overseer's favorite emotions in mortals.

While they fought the magic's unbreakable bonds, he busied himself dividing the bile into equal portions in smaller vials.

Lucky for him he always kept a basic alchemy kit with him. Nothing as elaborate as what an actual alchemist carried, but enough to get simple jobs done. Equally lucky, the poison had no effect on his already dead host body. If Overseer drank the stuff, it wouldn't bother him in the least. In fact, he sometimes did drink it, as the corruption strengthened the magic binding him to his host.

Now that his preparations were complete, Overseer went to the nearest mercenary, a battered, scarred man with a bald head and ragged equipment that the legion would melt down for scrap. Transforming this lout would be a favor.

When he loosened the ethereal bonds holding his jaw shut, the mercenary screamed bloody murder. Overseer let him carry on for a minute or two. They were far enough from the fortress that the White Knights on duty wouldn't hear anything. In fact, he doubted there were any other people for miles in any direction. Whatever source of corruption they found out here should be interesting. If it turned out to be just another bile pit, Overseer would be disappointed.

Of course, as long as the archbishop wasn't disappointed, nothing else mattered.

The mercenary had finally run out of lung capacity. Overseer bound his mouth wide open and poured the first small vial of Black Bile down his throat.

The poison flooded corruption through the man's body, shutting down his organs and killing him in moments. Overseer shook his head. The only problem with Black Bile was how quickly it claimed the victim's life. You just couldn't enjoy it when it ended so fast. At least the terror of seeing it coming could be drawn out.

He shrugged away his annoyance and got to work. At his command, ether flowed into the dead mercenary. Instantly the bile corrupted it. That served Overseer's needs perfectly. As a demon spirit, his abilities nearly doubled when using corrupted ether.

Half a minute of work sealed the bile inside the body, primarily by replacing the bone marrow. The flesh had already melted a little. No matter how fast he worked, Overseer never managed to avoid all damage to the host. In this case, that would work to his advantage. The bile zombies' horrific appearance increased the fear and horror of those opposing them.

He bared his teeth. Pity they were fighting White Knights. Those zealots made even the most devoted members of the cult look positively uncommitted in comparison. Overseer doubted even the most horrific monster would get them to break and run.

The first bile zombie complete, he moved on to the next trembling mercenary. The man had soiled himself. How distasteful. Oh well, Overseer had long since lost the ability to smell anything.

Performing the ritual over and over would have sent a human wizard into shock from the backlash, but Overseer handled it with only minor difficulty toward the end when the ether started to slip out of his control. No pain or exhaustion troubled him. Sometimes he felt like the ether simply grew offended if you used it for too long. Ludicrous, of course. An energy field felt nothing about anything. More likely his continuous use of magic affected his focus.

Even a demon had limits.

Despite his issues, he completed the last zombie successfully. Twelve bile zombies to conquer a heavily defended fortress manned by zealots with no concept of retreat.

His half-melted face twisted as it tried to smile. Should be entertaining.

———

Gaius stood on the battlement of the unnamed fortress and let the chill fall wind slap the sleep out of his eyes. His crisp, perfect, white uniform snapped in the breeze. He'd only earned his cloak three months ago. At the ceremony, his heart had filled with pride and his imagination with visions of glorious battle spreading the faith to heathen tribes.

Instead, he'd been ordered, along with a third of his cohort of new recruits, to man this fortress in the middle of nowhere. No explanations were offered or requested. A White Knight served where the church required. His preference played no part in the decision.

He blew out a breath and looked around. For at least twenty miles in every direction spread a forest of fine spruce and mixed hardwood. A forester could make a good living in a place like this.

It seemed strange that the empire hadn't sent any settlers to tame the wild country. As far as he knew, no native tribes called the area home either. That struck him as even stranger. Surely any tribes nearby would want to move into such a beautiful area.

All of that begged the question: if nothing lived out here besides deer and birds, why, in The One God's name, did the church build this huge fortress? They had nothing to defend against. He looked up at the beautiful blue sky and sent up a prayer that his posting here would be short. Of all the fates he'd considered before joining the White Knights, dying of boredom hadn't crossed his mind.

A faint sound came to him on the wind. Not a bird call. No bird that ever lived made a cry like that. He shivered and not from the chill air. Despite the complete lack of proof, deep in his soul he knew something evil made that noise. If felt like The One God himself whispered the warning into his ear.

Gaius couldn't ignore the feeling, though he doubted

subcommander Florens would be best pleased by him offering a report with nothing to back it up beyond a faint sound and a feeling, especially if he left his post.

Another noise, maybe a fraction louder, though that might have been his imagination, rode in on the wind. It sounded like a scream, shriller than the first noise he heard, but close enough that he felt certain the first noise had been a scream as well.

He stared into the forest, trying to figure out where the scream came from and more importantly what had made it. Try as he might, Gaius didn't think a human throat could produce such a sound, though he had visited the Inquisition briefly and the heretics certainly did scream.

"Gaius!"

He jumped so high he nearly fell off the battlement. Subcommander Florens stalked toward him, his craggy face scowling like a thundercloud. He wore a copper amulet with The One God's circle drawn on the surface. One day Gaius would like to earn one, but he had a long way to go to reach the same rank as Florens.

When he'd recovered his balance, Gaius snapped to attention. "Sir!"

"What part of 'always be on alert' did you not understand? I could have walked right up behind you and slit your throat before you knew what was happening. You're a disgrace to that cloak, Gaius. What do you have to say for yourself?"

"I'm sorry, sir. I heard something that sounded like a scream out in the forest and I was trying to figure out where it came from."

It seemed impossible, but Florens's frown deepened further. "That's madness, soldier. There's nothing out here but us and we're not due for a visit from the Inquisition until spring. You probably heard some animal getting killed and your imagination did the rest. You came out with the last cohort, right?"

"Yes, sir." Gaius debated dropping the matter, but felt like he needed to at least make one more effort to convince his commander. "Sir, I've heard animals when they're killed and they don't make a noise like what I heard. If you have a minute, it might come again."

Florens crossed his arms. "If you're wasting my time, so help me I'll see you stripped of your cloak and sent packing out of the White Knights."

"Thank you, sir." Gaius sent a silent prayer to The One God that the noise came again. He hadn't been a White Knight long enough to want to lose his post.

The seconds ground by and after thirty sweat plastered Gaius's tunic to his back despite the chill. Nothing would happen and Florens would bust him down to cleaning chamber pots. He kept up the slow count in his head. At fifty-five the scream drifted in again.

"There, sir," Gaius said.

Florens cocked his head and listened until the noise faded. "I grant you that it certainly sounded like a scream. Whether it's a threat to us or not is another matter. I don't know for sure, so I'm raising the alert level by one. Hopefully by the end of the day we'll know more."

When Florens turned on his heel and strode back the way he'd come Gaius's heart finally slowed to something approaching normal.

Florens spun back and pierced him with a final look. "Maybe you're not a complete screw-up."

Gaius hid his smile until his commander had really left. "Not a complete screw-up" was high praise from Florens. Suddenly Gaius didn't feel so bad about his prospects after all.

Mind considerably at ease, he settled in to keep watch. As he stood there staring out into the empty forest, Gaius couldn't make up his mind whether he wanted something to show up or if he preferred to be wrong. Some action would take the edge off his boredom, but it might also get some of his fellow knights killed. Being wrong might be better for everyone.

It took fifteen minutes for the second shift to hit the wall. When the alert level went up, the wall guard doubled and archers went to man the towers. The new arrivals spaced themselves equally between the men already on the wall. It showed the discipline of the White Knights that none of them grumbled a word of complaint.

Of course, if they had and Florens heard them… Gaius shuddered. He'd hate to be the unfortunate knight that ended up on Florens's bad side.

Two hours passed and Gaius began to think nothing would actually happen when the first figure shambled out of the forest directly across from his section of the wall. It looked like a mercenary dressed in leather armor, but it carried no weapon and he would have sworn that its—his?—face had melted a little. Gaius didn't think he'd ever seen or even heard of something so horrible.

One after another, more mercenaries stepped out of the forest. They all looked like a version of the first; leather armor, slightly melted face.

What the hell were they?

He looked left and right. No one spoke, but from their expressions he knew the others were worried. No doubt his own face held the same expression.

"Whoever you are!" Florens's voice boomed out. "You are trespassing on church ground. I'm giving you one chance, and one chance only, to turn around and go back to wherever you came from."

If the mercenaries heard or understood they gave no sign. Instead, they continued forward at a steady shamble.

Florens waited five seconds then said, "Archers, fire!"

Arrows arced out of the towers. A few ended up buried in the ground, but most hammered into the flesh of the mercenaries. After a few volleys they looked like pin cushions, but that didn't slow them down. They simply kept walking forward no matter how many wounds they took.

Gaius looked closer. They didn't bleed. The only thing that leaked out from around the arrows puncturing their flesh was some sort of black tar. Whatever these things were, they weren't men, at least not anymore.

"Cease fire!" Florens said. "Runner! Get the fortress commander up here, now."

The designated White Knight left his place at the wall and ran down the stone steps, across the training yard, and into the keep. Perhaps he imagined it, but Gaius thought he heard a hint of fear in Florens's voice. If true, that would be a first during his time at the fortress. Of all the firsts he'd hoped to see, this one sat at the bottom of the list.

The creatures, whatever the hell they were, had covered half the distance separating the fortress and tree line by the time Fortress Commander Cossus reached the battlements. The fortress commander had hair nearly as white as his cloak and a face covered in scars from many wars. Rumor said that Cossus had fought a dozen battles against the church's enemies. Commanding this fortress was supposed to be a reward for his lifetime of service.

It struck Gaius as more of a punishment.

Everyone turned to look at their leader. Cossus glared down at the approaching monsters and gave a slight shake of his head. Apparently he didn't like what he saw any better than Gaius did.

After a few seconds of study, he looked up and said, "It seems the enemy the church feared has finally arrived. Hear me well, men. These unholy creatures are the product of infernal magic. They seek nothing less than your death and to claim the demonic artifact we've been assigned to protect."

Gaius blinked. A demonic artifact? That's what the fortress protected? He'd had no idea and doubtless no one else had either. A million questions popped into his head, the most pressing of which being why, in The One God's name, did they hide something so important in the middle of nowhere? If they were closer to Tiber, they might be able to call for reinforcements. Out here, they were on their own.

"In The One God's name," Cossus continued. "We must stand here. We must stop these unholy brutes no matter the cost. When this battle is over, you will look back long years from now and know that this was the defining moment of your life. The One God is watching. Make Him proud."

Gaius stood up straighter, determination filling him. On either side of him the other White Knights responded to Cossus the same way. When the man spoke, you wanted nothing so much as to not disappoint him. He felt like an embodiment of The One God's will.

The sound of footsteps behind him heralded the arrival of knights loaded down with spears from the armory. Though White Knights favored the arming sword, they all trained with a variety of weapons, including spears. When one of the knights on the ground stopped under Gaius's position and handed up a spear, he took and hefted the weapon. It had a solid ash haft and leaf-shaped point. A good weapon, but he doubted how effective it would be against creatures able to shrug off a dozen arrows.

When all the knights manning the battlements had spears, Cossus said something to Florens prompting him to salute and jog to the opposite side of the wall.

The monsters were only fifty paces away now. Gaius frowned at them. How did the stupid things expect to climb the wall with no siege equipment? They didn't even have ropes or ladders.

"Take heart," Cossus said. "Though they are strong and tough, the monsters aren't invincible. Our brother warriors in the Second Legion have already fought and defeated many of the creatures. The process is a difficult one, especially given our defensive position, but it can and will be done."

Three figures without armor or weapons and carrying large satchels emerged from the keep. Gaius had never spoken with any members of the fortress's team of alchemists, but everyone knew them by sight. The three men wielded the Prophet's holy knowledge. Despite knowing almost nothing about alchemy, Gaius had seen the results of its power.

When the alchemists had joined him on the wall, the shambling creatures had halved the distance between them and the wall. A queasy feeling ran through Gaius. A sense of wrongness radiated from them even from this distance.

"Your job," Cossus said. "Is to keep the creatures out of the fortress. Don't try to kill them, even imperial steel is largely harmless to them. Let the alchemists and their holy fire destroy the abominations."

With that, the alchemists each pulled a vial out of their pouches and hurled them at the approaching creatures.

Explosions of flame sent the things flying and nearly blinded Gaius.

When his vision cleared, he found the blasted enemies climbing back to their feet, charred but otherwise little bothered.

The shambling pace from earlier must have been a ruse. When they regained their feet, the monsters sprinted for the wall.

They sprang, sank their fingers into the stone, and started climbing.

Gaius's throat tightened and he readied his spear. The wall was made of solid granite. How did they melt through it like that? And what would it do to his flesh if they got ahold of him?

Suddenly very glad for the reach of his spear, Gaius drew back and stabbed the creature in its half-melted face.

The spear tip punched through its cheek like nothing.

Unfortunately, "nothing" described the results of his attack equally well. It didn't even flinch when Gaius cut half its face off.

Out of the corner of his eye, Gaius caught glimpses of his fellow knights trying to hack apart the creatures nearest them. Looked like they weren't having any better luck than he was.

The thing had climbed within a few yards of the battlement lip when inspiration struck him. Gaius stabbed down at its fingers, severing first one hand then the other and sending it crashing back to earth.

He offered a silent prayer of thanks and shouted, "Their hands are their weak point! Go for the fingers!"

The words were passed down the line and in less than a minute every one of the brutes slammed into the ground.

Looked like round one to the defenders.

Gaius stared in disbelief as some kind of tar oozed out of the severed finger holes and formed into a new set of inky-black digits. The moment their hands were repaired, the creatures started climbing again.

How? Gaius's mind reeled. Were the things unkillable?

He dismissed the thought at once. If Commander Cossus said the Second had defeated them, then they were killable. Of course, he didn't say how much trouble they had or how many losses the legion sustained.

His focus turned at once to the monster quickly climbing into spear range. He steeled himself and prepared to slice the black digits off just like he'd severed the fleshy ones.

When he thrust down, the thing batted his spear away with the hand he hadn't targeted. Gaius frowned, drew back, and struck again. Again it warded him off.

They were in a standoff. It couldn't advance and Gaius couldn't cut it off the wall.

A scream sounded and he turned in time to watch one of his fellow knights get yanked off the wall by the monster he'd been trying to stab. He landed with a horrible crunch of broken bones.

Gaius had no time to mourn. His own opponent tried to do the same thing to him and only the warning he just received prevented it from succeeding. As it was, he barely jerked the spear back in time to avoid getting it snatched out of his hand.

Cursing the creature, he slashed with the spear head, taking its free hand off at the wrist before swinging back to hack the fingers holding on to the wall. Once more it crashed to the ground only to instantly begin healing.

One of the alchemists came running over and without a word hurled something down at the unmoving creature.

Gaius closed his eyes in anticipation of another explosion.

When no flash seared his eyes behind his lids, he opened them again and watched thick, brownish goo spread over the prone monster. Thrash as it might, the creature failed to free itself from the stuff the alchemist deployed.

"You did well fending it off," the alchemist said as he pulled another vial from his satchel.

He tossed the vial down and it shattered on the trapped monster. A second later the liquid burst into flames. It didn't explode like the first one; instead a roaring inferno engulfed the...

"What are those things, sir?" Gaius asked.

"I doubt anyone knows for certain, but the report we received from the capital called them bile zombies. Seems as good a name as any other."

Gaius shuddered. Bile zombies. That sounded as horrible as the reality of the creatures. Whoever thought up the name did a fine job.

While the alchemist prepared to pour a second vial down on the still-twitching zombie, Gaius glanced down the line to see how the rest of the knights fared. As his gaze shifted, he noticed movement.

Impossible! The knight dragged from the battlements appeared to be moving. He sat up, his broken neck snapping back into nearly the correct position, and he stood. Human eyes had been replaced with black pits. The undead knight shuffled over to the wall and started scratching at it like he thought he might rip it down with his bare hands.

"Sir, the body," Gaius said.

The alchemist glanced over. "I'd hoped that since he wasn't killed with the zombie's claws the body wouldn't rise. Assuming we survive, I'll need to make a note of what happened and send it to the capital. I'm finished with this one."

"Should I go help the others?" Gaius asked.

"No. If you move, it will create an opening in our defenses. Hold your station and keep watch. You might see something the otherwise embattled soldiers miss. And should more of those things show up, The One God forbid, you know what to do."

"Yes, sir."

Gaius hated leaving his fellow knights to fight alone, but he also knew that the alchemist was right. He'd done enough drills on siege defense to last a lifetime. Granted, none of those lessons covered dealing with nearly invulnerable zombies, but the basic principles still applied. Unless a position appeared in danger of getting overwhelmed, you held your station and waited for orders or more enemies.

Swallowing a sigh, he looked down at the burned remains of the zombie he'd helped defeat. The pieces still wriggled around, but there wasn't enough left of it to heal into a useful shape. He shook his head; absolutely unbelievable. If Gaius lived, he'd have a tale to tell his grandchildren.

Over the next fifteen minutes, the other knights sent the remaining bile zombies down for the alchemists to trap and burn. As they learned the monsters' tricks, the knights did better and better. They didn't even lose another man, thank The One God.

Gaius glanced away from the final bonfire toward the forest. As he did, a single figure stepped out of the tree line. This one wore robes instead of the rough leather armor. Looking at the... man gave Gaius chills. This had to be the leader.

"Commander!" Gaius pointed to the new arrival.

Cossus looked where he indicated and nodded. "Archers! Target the man near the forest. Don't stop until I tell you or he drops."

Arrows arced out from the nearest tower. A dozen were in the air before the first one reached the target. Or at least before the first one should've reached the target. A foot from the new arrival, the first arrow turned aside and hammered into a tree behind him. The rest of them did the same.

Twenty arrows surrounded the man before Cossus shouted, "Cease fire!"

A few seconds passed.

The man raised his hands and darkness gathered around them.

CHAPTER 3

Joran had never been so happy to see trees in his life. Granted, the ones looming in front of them had turned black, their limbs twisted, and none had a single leaf, but at least they were a break from the endless plain with its strange jutting stone columns. Hopefully trees meant water. And maybe something to hunt. If the others were as hungry as Joran, fresh meat would be welcome.

Mia kept looking around as if expecting to be attacked at any moment. They'd been following Grub for most of an hour and he'd assumed she would eventually calm down, but he'd assumed wrong. If anything, his soulmate appeared even more on guard than earlier. Joran wished she'd give him something specific to look for, but the two times he'd asked, she shook her head and said something was watching them. When he pointed out that they were alone and the bleak landscape made it nearly impossible for anything to hide in ambush she shrugged and said she knew what she felt.

While he trusted her completely, Joran didn't know what to make of her current behavior. If something wanted to attack them, he wished it would, so Mia could kill it and get back to normal.

"The water's just ahead." Grub stopped a few strides from the blackened trees. His face had gone pale under his beard and sweat soaked his brow. "I need to rest a few minutes. Even with the amulet, using this corrupted ether is exhausting. Thank you for the loan. I wouldn't have lasted five minutes without it."

Grub offered the amulet to Joran but he shook his head. "Hang on to it. I'm fine sharing Mia's protection and if we need magic, it will do you more good than me."

After a long look Grub tucked the amulet into his pocket. No one, it seemed, wanted to wear the thing. Since he had no idea what Samaritan might have done to it, Joran figured better safe than sorry.

While the geomancer rested, Joran walked over to the nearest tree for a closer look. It had the thick, deeply grooved bark of an old oak. The limbs were twisted and gnarled like an arthritic hand. Nothing about them gave the impression of good health. In fact, Joran didn't think a tree could even live without leaves yet these didn't seem dead.

He reached out to touch it, paused, and pulled his hand back. Maybe Mia's nerves were infecting him, but then again maybe she had the right idea.

"What do you make of them?" Joran had been so focused he didn't even notice Stoneheart walk up behind him.

"I have no idea what to make of any of this. I've never seen a landscape this twisted even in my nightmares." Joran looked up at the thick black clouds. "Hopefully the storm will break tonight and we can get a good look at the stars. I know enough astronomy to hopefully figure out where we are."

Stoneheart looked up and shook his head. "If that's a natural storm, I'll eat my axe."

Joran smiled. The centurion was probably right, but hope sprang eternal. "Speaking of your axe, could I trouble you to chop off the lowest branch? I want to see if the trees are rotten or there's live wood under the bark."

"Can't imagine anything that color being alive, but we can take a look."

Stoneheart drew his axe from the loop at his waist and swung at a three-inch-diameter branch about five feet off the ground.

The imperial steel axe bounced off with a clang like it had hit metal.

Impossible. Joran finally stepped in and touched the tree. An instant later he jerked his finger back. The tip had turned red like he'd burned it. Still, the brief contact told him a great deal. Despite its appearance it felt cool and smooth, just like metal. He understood now what the trees were made of.

"Mia, could you touch the tree with your sword, please?"

She came over and glared at the trees as if they were her enemy. "It hurt you."

"You can't blame an inanimate object for my foolishness. I'll put some burn cream on it momentarily. Please, touch the branch with your sword."

She finally did so. The instant the silver sword touched the tree it steamed and hissed, much like the black sword in Tiber.

"That's enough, thank you. It's made of the same metal as the black sword. Why anyone would make a tree of black iron I have no idea, but that reaction proves it."

Mia moved her sword away but didn't sheathe it. In fact, she hadn't sheathed it since they arrived. "This place is wrong in so many ways. We need to find a way home before the corruption turns us to black iron."

Joran thought that unlikely, but he didn't disagree with her basic premise. Getting out of this place would suit him very well indeed. Pity he had no idea how they'd go about it. He didn't even know where they'd ended up much less how to get back to Tiber.

Grub finally stood, putting an end to his ruminations. "I'm ready. What say we go find that water?"

"Good idea, but if the path leads us through this iron forest, everyone needs to make sure not to touch any of the trees. They'll burn your bare skin."

"It does." Grub had the amulet out again. "But there seems to be a path. A narrow, twisty one, but none of the limbs reach the edge."

They gathered behind Grub, Mia and Joran in the middle with Stoneheart bringing up the rear, and set out down a path so crooked it would have broken a snake's back to follow it. The tree branches crowded the path to such an extent that sometimes they had to turn sideways to pass between them. But they did make it through and after what Joran guessed was half a mile, the little group reached a lake that sat in a crater centered in a clearing surrounded by fallen metal trees.

The water looked clear despite sitting in a hole gouged into the black earth.

"What now?" Stoneheart asked.

"Mia, you're up," Joran said. "Put your sword into the lake and let it do its thing."

She obliged, thrusting her silver sword into the water.

No reaction. Unlike the trees, the water didn't so much as ripple.

Joran took out a pouch of revealing powder and sprinkled a little bit on the surface of the lake. It sparkled a little. Some magic was involved, but nothing he understood. He'd assumed that sitting in the corrupted earth would have tainted the water, but as far as he could tell, there was nothing wrong with it.

Only one way to be sure. He put the revealing powder back and took out a new, unused vial. Joran dipped his hand into the water and pulled the full vial out. It looked as clear and clean as any water he'd ever seen. His hand hadn't burned either, arguing strongly for no corruption.

He raised the vial to his lips, but Stoneheart stopped him. "Best let me take the first sip, my lord."

Joran would have argued, but didn't want to insult the loyal centurion. He handed the vial over and Stoneheart downed it in one go. So much for taking a sip.

Stoneheart smacked his lips. "Pretty good. It has a mineral taste I quite like. I'd prefer a mug of ale, but this isn't bad."

"You feel no ill effects?" Joran asked.

"No. In fact, the weight that's been crushing me has lifted. I feel better than I have since we arrived in this forsaken place."

Joran nodded, confused but pleased. "Let's fill our skins and look around for tracks. Any animals in the area will have to come here to drink. Maybe we can luck our way into some fresh meat."

When they'd drunk their fill and collected as much water as their skins would allow, they separated to look around. Well, the dwarves separated. Mia stayed right at Joran's side which suited him fine. After his drink he understood what Stoneheart meant. He felt lighter than he had in days. Only Mia seemed unaffected. She appeared every bit as twitchy as ever.

"Doesn't this feel wrong to you?" she asked. "A source of fresh water in this corrupt place has to be a trap."

"I don't think so. Did you notice how those trees were knocked over?" When she nodded, he said, "I'll wager at the bottom of that lake you'll find a meteor made of the same metal as your sword. That'll be what's keeping it pure and giving it the mineral taste. That's just a guess, mind you. We'd have to swim to the bottom of the lake to find out for sure and I have no desire to do so."

"Me neither."

Half an hour of searching revealed a total lack of tracks. The clouds showed no sign of breaking up and it was getting dark.

"We'll camp here tonight and start fresh in the morning," Joran said.

None of the weary quartet argued. They ended up hunkering down right beside the lake on an especially flat section of dirt. Hopefully the water's purifying properties would keep them safe during the night.

His backside had barely touched the dirt when Mia grabbed his shoulder. "Look."

He turned the way she pointed. From the edge of the still-standing trees three figures in black robes had emerged to face them.

Joran had no idea what they wanted, but men in black robes seldom meant anything good.

CHAPTER 4

From the shadows of the forest, Overseer watched the human pests destroy his bile zombies one after the other. Much as he hated to give them credit for anything, he couldn't deny that they did learn. No doubt the ones that defeated his army near Tiber had taught this bunch the best way to defeat his soldiers.

The process took nearly an hour and claimed the life of one White Knight, but finally the last zombie lay burned to a useless collection of twitching flesh. While he had hoped to succeed with the basic zombies, the humans weren't the only ones that had learned from their earlier encounters. His presence mitigated some of the zombies' weaknesses. Or perhaps it would be more accurate to say his magic did. He specialized in creating and controlling monsters. Time to give the humans a demonstration of his power.

Overseer stepped out of the shadows and into the light, letting the defenders take a good look at him. Soon enough arrows came streaking his way.

With a thought, an ethereal barrier formed around him.

The arrows deflected left and right leaving him without a scratch.

Even from the distance he felt their fear. Sweet nectar indeed.

Now to show them what he'd learned.

Overseer raised his hands and corrupt ether swirled around them. Threads shot out from his fingers and into the twitching corpses littering the ground in front of the fortress wall. They rose and crushed together, their flesh melding and reforming. The process gained momentum as he tapped into the remaining magic of the Black Bile in their bones.

The alchemists doused his slowly forming monster with liquid fire.

An effort of will shifted a fraction of the bile energy into a fireproof barrier. It slowed the transformation, but ensured that his creature lost no more mass. Overseer wanted it to be as huge and horrible as possible to better terrify the humans looking on.

Fear, he'd found, did wonders to keep mortals from focusing on anything beyond running for their worthless lives.

He kept the shield in place until the torrent of flames ended. Hopefully that meant an end to the alchemist's fire. No, to be honest, he knew that wasn't the end of the vile stuff. If there was one thing you could count on with imperials, it was that they always had more alchemist's fire.

At least the amalgamation had nearly finished forming. It looked vaguely like a spider only with way too many legs and a giant mouth in the middle that dripped Black Bile.

If that didn't break the White Knight's morale, he didn't know what would.

Gaius trembled and watched with growing horror as the corpses he'd thought defeated seemed to melt and reform into some new creature. He knew not what to call the thing. His mind balked at the very idea that it existed. Flesh and bone shouldn't behave that way. Such an abomination shouldn't exist under The One God's watchful gaze.

When the alchemists all poured liquid fire on the monstrosity, he hoped for a moment that it might die before having a chance to return to what passed for life. Instead, some barrier appeared and turned the alchemist's fire aside before it did much damage. Even Gaius understood that the man with the black hands had to be responsible. What he had trouble understanding was why he let the zombies get killed in the first place had he the power to stop it.

He shook his head and tried to still the trembling in his legs. Trying to understand the thinking of someone that would make something like the zombies or this new horror was a waste of time. No rational person had a hope of understanding such madness.

The river of fire finally stopped and behind it the monster had transformed into a central mass with skinny legs jutting in every direction. It looked a bit like a child's drawing of a spider, assuming the kid didn't know how many legs a spider should have.

"Steady, men!" Cossus bellowed. "This new challenge must be met with the same courage as the last one. Take heart and know that The One God and your brother knights stand with you. When it comes, use your spears to pry it off the wall. Work together and with all your might. All wizards have limits and when this one reaches his, we'll burn his creation in holy fire as it deserves."

The speech stiffened Gaius's spine and stopped his shaking.

The commander was right. They'd beaten the zombies earlier and they would beat this thing now.

The time to put his brave words to the test came moments later. The molten flesh stopped shifting and settled into something that looked reasonably firm. As soon as it did, the creature scrabbled forward, arms flailing as it scurried up the wall like the spider it resembled.

Knights rushed to stop it, Gaius among them. He felt certain that leaving his post would be the lesser risk.

He stabbed as soon as the black mass came within reach of his spear.

Like the zombies before it, this thing's flesh yielded easily to his blow.

The spear plunged a foot deep into the central mass.

It didn't even react to what would have been a fatal blow in any other adversary.

A skinny black leg lashed out.

Gaius ducked, nearly losing his head and actually losing his spear.

Not good.

He backed away from the other knights and drew his sword. If it got high enough to actually be hit with the blade, they were probably doomed, but Gaius meant to be ready all the same.

A minute later a thud sounded and the knights let out a cheer.

The cheer died a moment later when the sound of claws on stone filled the air. The monster had already begun climbing back up.

How were they supposed to hold it down long enough for the alchemists to burn it? There might have only been one monster now, but its size made it so much harder to deal with. He glanced at Cossus in the hopes of finding divine inspiration. What he found was the fortress commander stabbing away with a spear of his own.

How would he come up with a plan while fighting on the front line? However, having their commander fighting beside them did seem to buoy the other knights, and the alchemists had their heads together. Maybe they'd been assigned to come up with the plan while Cossus fought. Probably not a terrible idea since they were almost certainly the smartest people in the fort.

A scream rang out when a black leg reached up and wrapped around one of the knights, lifting him off the battlement.

Gaius charged and swung his sword.

The imperial steel edge bit deep, but didn't sever the limb.

He ripped his blade free and the cut scabbed over with a black seal.

Another strike hit the same spot and this time it felt like he'd struck iron.

A hint of movement in the corner of his eye provided his only warning.

He spun right so the monster's leg only clipped his shoulder.

The power of the blow sent him sliding along the battlement away from his fellow knights.

Gaius scrambled to his feet in time to watch another of his brothers get snatched up and dragged off the battlement. He hurried to the edge and peered over. The knight was pressed into the monster's central mass and absorbed, making the creature a little bit bigger.

Everyone they lost would only make their enemy stronger. In that regard, this monster acted much the same as the zombies earlier. He needed to let the commander know. Not that he suspected Cossus could do anything about it.

He sprinted toward the thick of the fighting.

A leg swung in his direction and he made a quick, ineffective slash at it.

The monster shrugged off the blow, but did swing away to find another target.

"Commander!" Gaius shouted when he got close.

Cossus disengaged and turned to look at him. "What is it, soldier?"

"That thing is absorbing our dead and getting bigger."

"I noticed, son, though I thank you for the warning." A scream heralded the loss of another knight. "I fear the wall is lost. Fall back! Collapse to the keep!"

Knights repeated the order and soon they gathered in a clump, their spears pointed toward the monstrosity that slowly pulled itself up and over the battlements. They retreated as a group down the steps and across the training yard. Without his spear, Gaius found himself in the center beside Cossus. Somehow the veteran managed to remain calm despite the chaos and rampaging monster.

Speaking of which, through the gaps in the formation the spider thing was visible as it climbed down the wall to the training yard. Its flesh shifted and here and there a familiar face appeared only to vanish a moment later.

A strangled noise slipped out.

"Steady, soldier," Cossus said. "Our brothers are with The One God now. What happens to their flesh means nothing."

"Yes, sir."

Though he understood Cossus's words to be true, mastering his emotions took everything Gaius had. He risked a glance back. Florens had the other wall guards gathered at the keep entrance.

"Subcommander Florens is ready for us at the keep gate, sir."

"Good. I doubt that thing will give us much time to get inside."

As if it heard them, the monster surged forward.

Its attacks held no particular skill, but their sheer power combined with the number of legs made it nearly impossible for the defenders.

Knights went flying despite the density of their formation. It didn't help that the creature feared their spears not in the least. Of the forty knights that left the battlement, half made it to the fortress gate.

The doors creaked as Florens's group opened them.

"Hurry, sir," Florens said.

Cossus ignored him and they maintained their steady retreat.

The knight directly in front of Gaius went hurtling, giving him his first close look at the monster since they left the wall. The central mass had grown by about a third and the legs looked bigger around. More faces covered its rubbery hide, forcing Gaius to look away. No matter what Cossus said, seeing his brothers' remains treated that way left him sick in mind and body.

He had no idea how, but Gaius swore he'd see that monstrosity destroyed.

When they reached the stone steps Cossus said, "Front rank, engage! Everyone else inside!"

Six knights charged, spears leading.

Gaius offered a silent prayer for their souls, turned, and sprinted through the doors.

CHAPTER 5

Joran stared at the figures in black that had emerged from the tree line not long ago. He had no idea what to make of them. They looked like humans, but from this distance and with them shrouded in robes, he had no way to be sure. The trio made no effort to come closer.

"What do you suppose they want?" Mia asked. She held her silver sword bare in her hand and looked ready for a fight. "Think it's a trap?"

Joran shook his head. "I doubt it. If they meant us harm, they'd have attacked at night when three of us would've been asleep. Approaching in broad, albeit dim, daylight implies they want to make peaceful contact. Can you sense anything about them, Grub?"

Grub had his hand in his pocket, doubtless clutching the silver amulet Joran had loaned him. "I can't tell. Something about them repels the ether."

Joran frowned. "What would cause that?"

"No idea. I've never seen anything like it. It appears that there's an actual barrier pushing the ether away from them."

A quick glance into the ether confirmed what Grub said.

Unfortunately, Joran knew so little about magic that he had no way to know what it meant and if the far more experienced Grub didn't know, then he didn't know what to think.

"Are we just going to stand here staring at each other or what?" Stoneheart asked.

"No, we're not. Let's go introduce ourselves." Joran managed a step before Mia slipped in front of him. "What's wrong?"

"If they're trying to lure us closer, better if I'm in front."

Joran certainly had no argument for that. "Okay, but don't start anything. We have no idea where we are or how to get back. These people might be a treasure trove of information."

"Don't worry, I won't. It just makes me nervous that they won't come any closer. If they really wanted a peaceful conversation, they should walk over under a white flag or something."

He shrugged. For all they knew, in this place a white flag might mean "slaughter the lot of them." Making assumptions about another culture was a good way to end up in a fight. Anyone that had studied imperial history knew that.

They set out across the blasted earth. As the four of them got closer, the new arrivals made no move to attack or withdraw. They simply stood there waiting for Joran and his companions to get within talking distance.

Speaking of which... Joran dug a combined translation and detect-deception potion out of his kit and drank it down. He grimaced and tossed the vial away. Disgusting stuff. If he ever got back to his lab, giving that a better flavor would go right to the top of his to-do list.

They stopped five paces away from the locals. All three of them wore some kind of metal gloves that made their hands look like they were made of iron. The nearest one flipped back his hood. His head appeared to be wrapped in some kind of black iron mask.

Joran looked closer. Impossible. It wasn't a mask or gloves.

The man was actually made of black iron. Were they human or some kind of construct?

"Greetings, outlanders," the metal man said in perfect Imperial. "We sensed the bile portal activate and came to see who had arrived. I am Bahesti. Welcome to what remains of the Black Iron Empire."

Joran stared stupidly for a moment. The people that lived in the Black Iron Empire were actually made of black iron? In all his research he'd read nothing about that.

He shook off his stupor and bowed. "Thank you. Though I must admit that we didn't come here on purpose. We somehow triggered the...bile portal, did you call it? It transported us here along with the man we were hunting."

Bahesti nodded. "I thought one of your number was missing. I imagine you have many questions. We have some as well. We would welcome you to our village."

Mia tensed and her anxiety hit Joran like a sledgehammer. She'd been so jumpy since they got here that he didn't know how to handle it yet. It clouded his thinking. He neither wanted nor knew how to distance his thoughts from hers, so he'd just have to adjust. Still, he wished he could feel whatever it was that had her so on edge.

"Not sure that's a good idea," Stoneheart said. "My people spent a long time as slaves of this bunch. Can't say as I'm anxious to experience that firsthand."

Joran offered a silent word of thanks to Stoneheart for providing him with the excuse he needed. "As you can see, my companions are understandably nervous about accepting your hospitality. Perhaps we could speak at our camp instead. We set up right next to that lake of clear water."

"Yes, we noticed." Bahesti's tone held a note of distaste. "Alas, our current condition prevents us from coming any closer to the lake as the mithril meteor at the bottom causes us considerable discomfort. Your lady friend's sword creates a similar feeling, though not nearly as bad given the far smaller quantity of mithril."

"You mentioned that word twice now. I thought the sword was made of some kind of alchemically treated silver. I've never heard of a metal called mithril." Joran turned to the dwarves. "Have you two?"

Stoneheart shook his head. "We've never dug anything like it up in the mines. If we had, someone would've talked about it."

"I'm not familiar with the metal either," Grub said.

"That doesn't surprise me," Bahesti said. "There's no natural source of mithril on this planet. At least none that we know of. Sometimes a meteor with a mithril core strikes the planet, like the one at the bottom of the pool. Others, like your sword, were brought here from another world."

"Another world?" That sounded insane to Joran.

"Indeed. As I said, we have much to discuss. Will you not come to our village so we can speak inside like civilized people?"

Grub snorted a laugh. "Nothing civilized about anyone from the Black Iron Empire."

Bahesti turned to the dwarves. "I admit my ancestors treated yours horribly. But look around. All that we built was destroyed by our hubris. Less than a hundred survivors of the old empire remain and all of us are cursed with these metal bodies. I assure you, we have been thoroughly punished for our myriad sins. None of us have any desire to take slaves. We have no need of them in any case. Our bodies require no sustenance. We need no sleep and we can see but no longer touch the magic."

For some reason the potion didn't react to Bahesti's words one way or the other. Perhaps the potion didn't work because the ether couldn't touch him. Whatever the case, Joran had to make a decision without the aid of alchemy. He knew no one would like it, but they really needed information and it seemed Bahesti had it.

"Very well," Joran said. "We'd be delighted to see your village."

"Excellent." Bahesti's iron face showed no emotion, but from his tone Joran decided he was pleased. "Follow us."

Bahesti and his silent companions turned back the way they'd come. Mia inched up beside him as they walked and whispered, "Are you sure this is a good idea?"

"I'm sure of absolutely nothing beyond the fact that we're stuck here and these people are our best and perhaps only source of information. I am totally open to suggestions if anybody has one."

Mia's frown of concern didn't lessen, but she shook her head while both dwarves remained silent.

At least Bahesti led them down a path wide enough to make the walking easy. The branches of the black iron trees didn't even come close to reaching the path. Maybe they had some way of trimming them back.

"Your friends don't say much," Joran said in the hope that a little small talk might get the information flowing early.

"They are not friends," Bahesti said. "They aren't even alive. My guardians are black iron golems. Some of the few automatons to survive the apocalypse. The few survivors are scattered all over the empire. Only ten live in my village. We keep in touch through messenger automatons. Nowhere near as useful as magical communication, but given our current circumstances, the best we can manage."

"Why not get together and pool your resources?" Joran asked.

"You've seen the state of our land. Getting from one island to the next is no simple task, especially for people made of iron. Jumping is not our specialty. Other groups have other tasks. Some search the ruins of our once-great cities for anything useful. Two others watch bile portals like the one that brought you here. Mostly we just putter and try our best to stave off the endless boredom that is the worst part of our curse."

Bahesti turned forward, putting an end to the conversation. Despite everything Joran knew about what the Black Iron Empire had done, he found himself pitying the unfortunate fellow. Perhaps he had simply gotten what he deserved for his crimes; Joran didn't know enough about the man to say. Some certainly thought the people of the Tiberian Empire deserved exactly the same fate, but Joran knew many ordinary citizens who harmed no one as they strove to survive each day. Perhaps Bahesti had been innocent of any crime and simply got unlucky.

Joran swallowed a smile at his foolishness. No farmer struggling to make a living knew how to control a golem and they certainly wouldn't know anything about a bile portal. No, Bahesti was apt to be an imperial wizard, which probably meant he was evil to the core. That would have to be Joran's assumption until he knew for sure otherwise.

Half an hour of walking brought them to the edge of the metal forest. About a mile distant, scores of broken towers jutted into the sky. Some of them had to be fifteen stories tall. Even the biggest tower in Tiber didn't begin to compare. And like everything else he'd seen, the towers appeared to be made of black iron.

"This is your village?" Mia asked.

Bahesti chuckled. "Hardly. What you see used to be the provincial capital of this sector."

Joran's jaw dropped. "This is a provincial capital? I assumed it was the imperial capital."

"No, the Iron City is no more. If I were to take you to the capital all you'd find is a still-smoking whirlpool in the middle of the ocean. Of course, the fumes would kill you all in seconds, even with the protection of mithril. That once-glorious city is now nothing but a memory that lives in the minds of a few score cursed men and women. It would be best for the world if it were forgotten forever."

"You're wrong," Joran said. "The world needs to know what happened here, if only so we can stop it from ever happening again."

"There is wisdom in your words, young man."

"Joran. The young lady is Mia. The dwarves are Grub and Stoneheart."

"Pleasure to meet you all." He sounded sincere. After however many centuries he'd been wandering around a dead city with only other old metal men for company, any new arrivals must have made a welcome change of pace.

A black dirt road led to the city and made for easy walking. Happily, no metal trees loomed over the road. When they got out of here, Joran hoped to never see anything made of black iron for the rest of his life.

They walked down a broad thoroughfare through the shadows cast by the towers. There seemed to be nothing in the way of smaller buildings. Shops, houses, anything the suggested normalcy was absent.

"Where did the people live?" Joran paused to look at the huge empty spaces between the towers.

"There were smaller buildings once. They didn't survive the apocalypse. I think the husks of the towers were spared to taunt us. They serve as reminders of what we accomplished and lost." Bahesti shook his head. "A minor cruelty compared to some."

Ten minutes later they reached a sad, crude collection of six huts that appeared made of slabs of iron gathered from the smashed towers. A black metal head poked out of one of the huts, took one look at them and disappeared back inside.

"Not very friendly," Joran said. "If life is as boring as you describe, I figured the rest of your companions would be eager to join the conversation."

"Some of my people were… damaged by the transformation. Their minds don't work correctly anymore."

"Hardly surprising if their brains were turned to metal," Grub muttered.

Joran wanted to slap the dwarf in the head, but Bahesti just chuckled, a hollow, echoing sound devoid of humor.

"I'm not surprised you find pleasure in our circumstances. Of all the peoples we conquered, my ancestors treated yours the worst. Granted, not a lot worse, but still." Bahesti stopped in front of one of the huts. "My humble home."

He motioned them inside but Joran hesitated. Being surrounded by walls of corrupt black iron didn't strike him as a particularly healthy idea.

"If you have chairs, perhaps you could bring them out and we could sit here."

"Furniture, alas, is in short supply." Bahesti waved his golems off and dropped to the ground. "This, I fear, is the best we can do."

Joran and his companions sat in a semicircle facing Bahesti. Mia kept her sword bare and rested it across her legs so part of the blade touched Joran's knee. The contact made him feel instantly better.

Bahesti leaned forward. "Now, let me tell you about the end of my world."

CHAPTER 6

When the heavy wooden gate slammed shut, Gaius took his first easy breath in what felt like days. As he stood panting, bent double, four knights wrestled a foot-thick beam into a massive bracket forged from imperial steel. Gaius hesitated to think it was impossible for the monster to get inside, but it would certainly be a difficult task.

Most of the knights that had fought with him on the wall lay on their backs staring up at the ceiling. Only Cossus remained on his feet, pacing and muttering. His furious expression alone would have balked most enemies, though Gaius doubted it would do much to dissuade the creature outside.

A heavy blow rattled the door, but it didn't otherwise budge, thank The One God.

Cossus rounded on the alchemists. "How do we kill it?"

The three alchemists huddled together as if afraid to draw his wrath. At last the man in the middle, the oldest if Gaius was any judge, hesitantly said, "The thing is, sir, we don't know. All the information we had applied to the human forms of the monsters. This new, larger shape, combined with the demon magic of the one controlling it, makes it an even greater threat.

We may have to accept the simple truth that we're in over our heads."

"Perhaps if we get word to the capital, the alchemists there will have some suggestions," one of the other alchemists offered.

"You think that wizard will just let a messenger bird escape?" Cossus demanded.

The man who made the suggestion shrank away from him. "It was just a thought, sir."

Cossus waved a hand. "I know. My anger isn't directed at you, but the situation."

Another blow buffeted the door. Despite rattling the bar, the blows seemed to cause no damage. Somehow Gaius doubted that would last.

"Does anyone have any suggestions beyond just trying to escape?" Cossus looked around, almost pleading with his eyes.

Unfortunately for him, no one had any answers. And escaping would be no simple thing. As far as Gaius knew, there was no hidden tunnel or other secret way of getting out. Only the fortress's main gate allowed entry and exit. Convenient for defense, but a major issue if you needed to get out without drawing attention.

"Can't we fight our way past that thing and flee?" a knight asked. Gaius couldn't tell who spoke. The man probably didn't want to be accused of cowardice. Though who would make such an accusation under these circumstances, Gaius had no idea.

"If we run," Cossus said. "That monster and its master gain the demon artifact. We were all assigned to this fort to prevent that from happening. Running would be a total dereliction of duty. Would any of you be able to face The One God knowing you abandoned your duty?"

The knights all looked away as if ashamed. For his part, Gaius stayed silent. The truth was, if they had no way to stop that thing outside, their deaths would be meaningless and the enemy would still gain the artifact. If they escaped, they'd have a chance to return and reclaim the fortress.

Not that he had the nerve to say that to Cossus.

"Whatever you decide, we're with you, sir," Florens said.

Murmurs of agreement met that statement though with little enthusiasm. To a man they knew that to stay and fight meant death. Even the knowledge that you'd receive your eternal reward for loyal service did little to make a man excited to face certain death.

"We'll hold out as long as we can," Cossus said. "The gate seems to be holding and there's no other way something as big as that monster can get in here. If worst comes to worst, we fall back to the basement and hold them off as long as possible. Gaius, come here."

Gaius nearly leapt out of his boots when Cossus called him over. "Sir?"

"I have a special mission for you. Walk with me."

Gaius followed the older man out of the main hall and down one of the many smaller halls deeper into the keep. Cossus didn't speak for what felt like a long time as they walked. An air of melancholy seemed to radiate from him.

At last, he stopped and turned to face Gaius. "What I'm going to ask of you won't be easy. It goes against everything you've been taught as a White Knight, but it is important."

"Whatever you need, sir, I'll do my best." Gaius tried not to let his anxiety show and feared he failed miserably.

"I know you will. You proved a keen observer during the battle and this task requires brains and stealth, not brawn." Cossus took a deep breath and blew it out. "When that creature breaks through, and it will eventually, I have no doubt, I need you to escape and get word to the pope. His Holiness will know best what must happen next."

"The pope?" The question came out as a squeak. "Will anyone even let me speak to someone so high-ranking?"

"They will when you show them this." Cossus pulled a gold amulet out of his pocket. The One God's crimson circle was prominent on the front. "There are only ten in the world. It marks the bearer as someone of the highest rank in the church. If nothing else, someone will want to know how you ended up with it. When you tell them what happened here, I guarantee His Holiness will want to talk to you."

Gaius hesitantly held out his hand and accepted the surprisingly heavy amulet. The weight of the responsibility Cossus placed on him made it feel even heavier. He understood that his brother knights were going to die and that if he failed this mission, he would be failing all of them as well, rendering their deaths meaningless. Much as he wanted to live, dying almost felt like the easier option.

"I won't let you down, sir."

Cossus clapped him on the shoulder. "I know you won't. That's why I chose you for this mission. Now, let me show you how you're going to escape."

———

Overseer smiled a twisted, lopsided smile. At last, the miserable humans had broken and run. Now he just needed to finish the job and find out what they were trying so hard to protect. While his bile beast chased the survivors across the courtyard, Overseer strode across the killing field toward the fortress.

Every step made the source of corruption feel stronger. He had no idea what awaited him inside, but doubted it was anything so simple as a bile pit. This felt stronger by several orders of magnitude. Well, whatever it was, his mistress would be pleased when he offered it to her on a silver platter. And anything that pleased the archbishop pleased him as well. Mostly because she'd be less likely to send him back to Hell.

At the wall, he used the ether to lift himself up and over. He landed just in time to watch his creation flailing uselessly against a closed gate. So the knights had made it to safety. Or at least what they imagined to be safety. A gate of metal and wood, no matter how well made, would serve only to slow him.

At Overseer's mental command the bile beast stopped its useless pounding and moved back a few paces. He closed his eyes and ran a hand over the wood. Probes of ether shot out, meeting no more resistance passing through the gate than they did the air. He felt the knights' fear and anxiety and licked his lips. They were beaten, they just hadn't accepted it yet.

Good, that would make slaughtering them all the more entertaining.

He pointed at the gate and the bile beast put five of its legs against it.

A blade of ether lashed out, slicing through two of the legs. Black bile oozed out and Overseer's magic seized it, smearing the black tar against the wood, and charging it with corrupt energy. The wood began to rot instantly.

Overseer gave the process a few more seconds, both to make sure the wood got good and punky and to let the knights inside tremble for just a little bit longer.

When he felt certain no structural integrity remained, he pointed at the gate.

The bile beast charged, hitting the gate like a battering ram and sending pieces of wood flying in every direction.

Despite their fear, the knights inside did a credible job forming up and retreating in good order. Not that they really had anywhere to retreat to since Overseer and his monster blocked the only exit.

Instead, they went deeper into the building. None of the knights made any attempt to counterattack. They contented themselves with blocking any strike the bile beast might make.

If their goal was to not get hit, they succeeded far beyond his expectations. Winning, however, would be an impossibility.

Of course, even if they attacked, winning would have been impossible given their weapons and lack of real magic.

Overseer grimaced and forced himself not to get too confident. Last time he did that, it cost him his base of operations and his mistress's goodwill. Despite their weakness, underestimating humans never led to anything good.

The halls began to narrow the deeper they went into the keep. The bile beast knocked suits of armor off their stands and smashed paintings as it forced itself down the hall.

Was this their plan? Lead his monster to a passage narrow enough to limit its attacks before they made their move? Not a terrible idea, but of course they didn't fully understand everything his beast could do.

A bit of magic injected into the bile running through the beast's body changed its shape into something narrower and longer. It still smashed everything it passed, but now it did so for pleasure rather than necessity.

At the end of the hall waited yet another door. The knights continued their retreat down the steps beyond it.

Overseer smiled. This had to be it. The corruption radiating out of that door nearly made his head spin. More power than he'd ever encountered seethed in the basement of this place. It amazed him that the humans survived in such close proximity to it.

His smile curdled. Peering through the ether it became instantly clear the threads of corruption totally avoided the humans. Instead, they went into the bile beast. For a moment he figured they were strengthening his monster. But that fiction collapsed when a shudder ran through the beast.

By the narrowest of margins, he conjured an ethereal shield before the monster exploded, showering him with bits of gore. If that's how undead flesh reacted to the corruption downstairs,

Overseer had no desire for a closer look. Uncontrollable power as apt to burn the hand seeking to control it as the target was of little value.

Overseer pointed at the open basement door. It slammed shut, trapping the knights in the basement. A simple binding spell would serve to keep them there until he contacted his mistress and explained the situation.

The archbishop could figure out what was going on. And if she couldn't, then he doubted anyone in the world could.

―――――

Gaius stood in a specific, unused room on the second floor of the fortress. That no one used it came as no surprise given that it measured at most six-by-six square. He doubted a standard cot would fit. Not that the size mattered, what did, according to Cossus, was the arrow slit. Specifically, that it measured just wide enough for a slender man wearing no armor to force his shoulders through. From the outside, you'd hardly be able to tell the difference.

The second most important thing in the room was the iron ring hammered into the wall. Gaius had already tied a length of rope to it and given a hard yank to make sure it wouldn't go anywhere. This room had only one function: to let a single knight escape should the worst happen and word needed to reach the capital. The weight of the responsibility lay heavily on Gaius. If he failed, his brothers would have died for nothing.

A thunderous crunch from below signaled the end of the fortress gate. He took a deep breath to steady himself and started to count backwards from ten.

When he reached zero, the rope went out the arrow slit and down to the training yard with his sword and a survival pack tied to the bottom. Steeling himself, Gaius put his head out the opening, grabbed the rope, and pushed with all his might. After a moment of excruciating pain, he popped out, bracing himself with his legs on the fortress wall while holding the rope with his left. His right arm hung useless at his side. Something in his shoulder had given when he passed through the arrow slit.

Climbing down with only one hand had to make the list of most difficult tricks he'd ever managed. He collected his sword and slid it into the baldric at his waist. Like all White Knights, he'd learned to wield his sword in his off hand. Not well, but good enough to protect himself from a weak opponent.

The survival pack he slung over his shoulder. It held enough preserved food for two weeks along with a water skin. Not nearly enough to see him through to Tiber, but enough to give him a start anyway. Cossus had slipped him a small pouch of silver before leaving him in the escape room. If he got desperate, he could always buy more supplies at the nearest town.

Ignoring the pain, he worked his way around the fortress until he got close enough to peek around the corner at the gate. The thick wood-and-steel doors lay in chunks of rotten rubble. If he hadn't seen it with his own eyes, Gaius wouldn't have believed anything short of a battering ram would bring down that gate.

It really drove home just how powerless normal men were in the face of demon magic.

Speaking of which, he saw no sign of the wizard or his monster. Time to make himself scarce before they finished up and came hunting for strays.

He ran toward the outer gate, unbarred the sally port, and sprinted for the tree line. Only when the fortress had vanished behind the trees did he pause and catch his breath. A quick glance at the sun oriented him and he was on his way at a steady trot.

The capital waited and he had a long ways to go.

CHAPTER 7

Fane hadn't visited Beastmaster face-to-face in a long time. The boy made her uncomfortable. She didn't fear him. She didn't fear anyone on this world. Maybe it was the fact that he looked twelve, yet Fane had known him for better than four centuries. Beastmaster had studied with one of the other apprentices that came with the arcane lords when they first arrived on this world. He'd proved his worth by killing his master and taking the man's place.

Now only he and Fane remained. She shook her head as she walked down the crude stone tunnels. Beastmaster hadn't bothered to smooth the walls of his home. When she'd asked him about it once he just cocked his head and asked what the point would be. He didn't need the walls to be smooth; he needed them strong and they were.

She never brought the matter up again, but the aesthetic offended her. She liked beautiful things with smooth, clean lines. Hours of effort had hidden all the seams where the stones of her citadel came together. It made absolutely no difference to anyone but her and she didn't care. Being immortal meant you had all the time in the world. Why shouldn't your home be as pleasing as possible?

"You okay?" Beastmaster looked up at her. "Your mind looked about a thousand miles away. Usually when you come for a visit, you're more focused."

She grimaced, baring her needle-sharp eyeteeth. "I'm a bit frustrated at the moment. I have agents on the move, but I haven't heard from either of them. When I tried to contact Samaritan, the link failed. Either he's lost the amulet or he's dead. Nothing else could keep me from reaching him. One of my overseers is investigating a powerful source of corruption on the coast. I expected him to have dealt with the guardians and reported back to me about the power source by now."

"Is that the same one that screwed up in Tiber? I can't keep the ugly things straight."

His reminder of her servant's failure did nothing to improve Fane's mood. She flicked a glance at the youthful-looking wizard as he marched along beside her in his slightly too big brown robe. Beastmaster didn't say these things to anger her, he simply didn't seem to think through the potential results of his comments. Probably because he spent too much time around animals.

"Yes," Fane said at last. "It's the same one. And if he screws up again, I'll replace him with a new demon spirit."

"That's such a pain. I used demon spirits for a while, but found most of them so stupid they weren't much more use than my pets. Anyway, that guy you didn't want me to kill is in a pit up ahead. I'm glad you finally came to talk to him. Keeping the weakling alive took way more effort than I wanted to expend on a human."

Beastmaster waved a hand and a section of the tunnel wall vanished. Beyond it a huge cavern sprawled out in about a fifty-yard oval. Four pits five yards across dotted the floor. Beastmaster led her to the nearest one.

At the bottom a figure dressed in a white cloak lay in the hay that lined the floor of the pit. He didn't even look up at their approach.

"I said to keep him alive."

"He is alive. Watch, he'll twitch or cough or something any second now." As if he heard Beastmaster speaking, the human coughed and rolled over to stare up at them. "See, he's alive. Now if you'd just ask him whatever you want to know, I'd be very happy to make him not alive."

She shot Beastmaster a glare. He was getting a little snippy. Had the time come to remind him again which of them was the greater power? Much as she would have enjoyed doing exactly that, with so many pieces in the air she didn't dare risk him breaking into open rebellion. Defeating him in a real battle, one where Beastmaster actually exerted his full power, would leave her weak for days if not weeks.

No, that reckoning would have to wait until matters settled. Despite his childlike appearance, Beastmaster wasn't blind or incompetent. He might well have been pushing her simply because he knew he could get away with it right now.

"He will stay alive until I tell you otherwise." Fane hopped over the edge of the pit and landed easily beside the groaning human. "I have questions. You will answer them or you will be punished. Understand?"

The human rolled his eyes and looked about ready to pass out. Beastmaster might have kept him breathing, but the prisoner was useless in this condition.

Fane grabbed him by the tunic and hoisted him to his feet. Her undead body granted her strength far in excess of what her slender body should possess. His eyes opened and when his gaze locked with hers he stiffened as her innate ability to control the minds of mortals kicked in. A thin trickle of ether strengthened his body and mind. That should be enough to get at least a few answers out of him.

"Tell me about Samaritan," she said.

"Bellator was my friend and hero. He represented everything I believed a White Knight should be. Our superiors betrayed him and sent mercenaries to kill him. They failed, but did kill his soulmate. He hates the empire and the church. I thought he'd lost his way, but the more I learn, the more I think we might be the ones that lost our way."

Fane clenched her jaw. She knew all that already. "Do you believe he could be turned aside from his goal of destroying the empire?"

"I doubt it. So much hate in him now. I felt it when he looked down at me before cutting the rope. Hate and maybe a little sadness."

Sadness? She didn't like the sound of that. Hate she trusted, but sadness made your insides weak.

"What was he sad about, killing you?"

The human shook his head, whether in denial or uncertain she couldn't say, and fell unconscious despite the magic she used to keep him upright. Fane dropped him back to the hay and leapt out of the pit.

"He's useless like this. Heal him and restore his strength. He might come in handy should Samaritan actually harbor some sort of fondness for him."

Beastmaster waved a hand at the cold cavern. "I'm not exactly set up to run a hospital here. Wouldn't you rather take him to your citadel?"

Fane shook her head. "Too much corruption and too many undead wandering around. His life force would be snuffed out in a couple days. No, you're going to have to be his keeper for a little while longer. When I come back, I expect him healthy and strong enough to hold a proper conversation. I—"

She stopped as soon as she sensed her overseer attempting to make contact. The connection felt strange, like something was trying to keep her from completing the link. Her eyes narrowed as she concentrated, trying to force the ether to do what she wanted.

After a full minute it became clear that she'd need the crystal ball in her casting chamber to get the chaos sorted out.

"I have to go. You know what you need to do."

"I hope your servant has good news." To her surprise, Beast-master sounded like he meant it.

Fane became one with the ether and a moment later appeared in her casting chamber. The buzz in the back of her mind remained steady but hazy and indistinct. She'd never felt anything quite like it, especially not when a demon she summoned herself attempted to contact her.

Shaking off her annoyance, Fane strode over to the head-sized crystal ball resting on a black iron tripod. She laid her fingers on the smooth surface and tried again to establish a connection. This time the link formed, but she still didn't see the overseer in her crystal ball.

"Report."

"I control the fortress, but there's a problem." The next sentence came through garbled. "Can't gain access to the power source. It destroyed my bile beast and if I get too close I fear it might do the same to me. Please advise."

Fane frowned. A source of corruption that destroyed rather than strengthened undead? She'd never even heard of such a thing. Her long-dead heart jumped. Finding something she'd never heard of excited her a great deal.

"Has the sun set there?"

"Yes, Mistress."

"Okay, move far enough away from the power source that the interference won't ruin my spell and I'll join you momentarily."

"If I leave, the humans may escape. About twenty of them have taken up refuge in the fortress basement."

Fane kept her patience firmly under control. "Set a death

ward in the doorway. If the first one that tries to leave dies, the rest will take the hint. Now move!"

His mental flinch made her smile as she released the spell. She rubbed her hands, eager for the challenge. Whatever she found, it was certainly going to be interesting.

CHAPTER 8

Sitting in the dirt outside a hut made of corrupt black iron didn't make for the most comfortable situation, but Joran found himself leaning forward, eager to hear Bahesti's story. He'd read a little about the Black Iron Empire during his research, but all of it came from secondhand sources and educated guesses. And not terribly educated ones at that. Hearing the story right from the mouth of someone that lived it was a dream come true for a scholar.

"Greed destroyed us," Bahesti said. "The empire sought power above all things and we weren't particular where it came from. The overmages would bargain with demons without a second thought. But our greatest source of power came from Black Bile."

"Who were the overmages?" Grub asked.

"Our rulers, the strongest wizards in the empire. Any wizard could challenge an overmage and, if they won, take the vanquished's place on the Council of Twelve. Doesn't matter now. They're all dead, destroyed when Iron City fell."

Joran shot Grub a look he hoped made clear his desire to avoid further interruptions. "You were saying about the Black

Bile? We've run into undead creatures that have it running through them like blood, and I know it's an especially potent poison. Are there other uses for it?"

Bahesti chuckled. "There are so many uses for it that your head would spin. Assuming, of course, that you have no ethics or concerns about manipulating essentially liquid evil. That's what Black Bile is, concentrated corruption given physical form. We used it to power our magic and transform normal metal into black iron. I will grant you that our black iron is inferior in every way to the stuff the demons make in their Hell forges, but it is far stronger and more durable than anything else you'll find on this world."

"How can you use it?" Mia asked. "I touched a black iron sword and it burned my fingers."

"We used a special leather to wrap the handle. And even then, our black iron would only sting, not burn you. I suspect the weapon you encountered was a Hell-forged blade. Very rare and valuable. Also evil and soul corrupting. But plenty of people wouldn't care about that."

"So the Black Bile became an important source of power for the empire," Joran said, trying to get the conversation back on course. "What did that have to do with your fall?"

"Everything. The overmages weren't content with the bile that naturally bubbled up and decided to seek the source. Well, they found it. Black Bile is a sort of slime that oozes off the scales of this world's guardian dragon. It sleeps in the earth most of the time and the bile slowly works itself up to the surface. Of course, the overmages didn't know that when they went looking. I have no idea what they expected to find, perhaps some sort of hellgate, but when they found the dragon, they woke it up. The dragon destroyed Iron City before unleashing its wrath upon the entire world. All our cities fell, even the smaller outposts took damage."

"One moment," Joran said. "You called this beast our world's guardian dragon. What sort of guardian creates chaos like you described?"

Bahesti shrugged. "A poor one, apparently. I know next to nothing about the beast beyond what the overmages called it and that it served as the source of the bile. Anyway, after shattering our continent, the dragon corrupted everything, transforming it into black iron. Then it vanished, back into the earth I assume, to return to its interrupted slumber."

The story made Joran's mind reel. It also revealed Samaritan's ultimate plan. The giant beasts were only the beginning. He had to be searching for a way to wake the dragon and use it to take revenge on everyone and everything he felt betrayed him.

Joran couldn't say exactly why he thought that, but something, some intuitive leap, insisted it was the truth. From what he'd just heard, they absolutely couldn't fail to stop him.

"Do you know where the dragon is now?" Joran asked.

"Not a clue and I'm happy to remain ignorant." Bahesti looked him dead in the eye. "That dragon is a cursed thing. No one should know where it lies. Better for the world if it remains asleep forever."

"I don't disagree," Joran said. "Unfortunately, the man we were chasing is, I believe, looking for the dragon's lair with the goal of waking it."

"That's insane."

Joran nodded. "Yes. Insane describes Samaritan's plans very well. Now that I know what he's up to, finding and capturing or killing him is my highest priority. Will you help us?"

"Help you find a man mad enough to seek the dragon of corruption? You may depend upon it. Heaven knows what it might do should someone wake it again."

"Thank you. Earlier you mentioned other groups. Would it be possible to warn them about Samaritan as well?"

Bahesti looked away. "That may not be wise. Some groups

would believe as I do and seek to help. Others, alas, have different views on the matter. Since we are now made of black iron, some see no great danger from the dragon. Yet others worship it as our creator and might well seek to aid this man in his quest."

Joran kept his expression smooth, but inside he seethed. So much for finding more help. "I see."

"I believe you do. Even among the fallen you will find madmen. I wonder sometimes if that isn't a failing of our species, whether made of flesh or metal."

"It certainly seems that way, doesn't it? Where should we begin searching?"

"I can draw up a rough map of the area. For now, you should rest. It will be fully dark soon."

"That's an excellent idea. We'll go back to the lakeshore to camp and return here at first light."

Bahesti's lips twisted in an approximation of a smile, the first show of emotion Joran had noticed on his iron face. "You don't trust me."

"No. If our positions were reversed, would you trust me?"

"Almost certainly not. Perhaps it will help if I explain what I want in exchange for my help." At Joran's nod Bahesti said, "I want your companion to use her sword to end my life. Nothing less than a mithril sword will do the job."

"You want Mia to kill you?"

"Yes. I weary of this life. Centuries of endless darkness and decay are nothing I would inflict on my worst enemy. I ask nothing else in exchange for my help."

"If your help includes a way back to our empire, you have a deal."

"There are other, still operable, bile portals. One of them might lead to your homeland. All are labeled for those that know how to read the overrunes."

"And you do?" Grub asked, his suspicion clear.

Bahesti nodded. "In life, I served as a scribe to a wizard with ambitions to the Council. Had I been unable to read the runes, I would have been of little use to her."

Joran stood and the others followed his lead. "We'll discuss your proposition tonight and let you know our decision when we meet in the morning."

Bahesti stood and bowed. "Fair enough. Good evening."

As soon as Bahesti stepped into his hut, Joran and his companions set out for the lake. Grub took the lead and led them unerringly back the way they'd come. Joran stayed silent the whole way, his mind racing.

Everything depended on getting this decision right.

———

Samaritan staggered away from one of the many pillars of dark stone that dotted the blackened earth of this island. As soon as he determined which way his hunters went, he'd chosen another path. Not directly opposite as that way led to a cliff with a hundred-foot drop that ended upon jagged rocks and crashing waves. No magic he knew would allow him to survive that fall and even if by some miracle he did, he saw no land on the horizon.

No, getting crushed or drowning hadn't appealed to him. Luckily, he found a path made up of more jutting pillars that led to another island. The first jump had to be twenty feet which explained why his enemies had chosen another way. Lucky for him, a little magic had made the jump doable if not easy.

Now he found himself on another island with no food or water. And worst of all, without his amulet he couldn't teleport back to his tower.

The overcast sky had threatened rain all day, but so far nothing besides lightning had fallen from the clouds. The idea that dehydration might kill him after all he'd survived nearly made him laugh... or cry. He couldn't quite decide which.

The shadows had lengthened a great deal. Sunset must be close, not that he could see the sun given the clouds. In all his travels Samaritan had never seen such dense cloud cover. It had to be magic, but when he peered at the clouds through the ether, he saw nothing that explained the bizarre weather, only masses of corruption.

Shaking off the pointless speculation, he trudged on toward what looked like black trees not so far away. He had no particular hope of finding anything useful there, but a forest usually meant animals. Maybe he'd cut a game trail that led to water.

He chuckled to himself. Amazing how the mind lied. He hadn't seen anything living since he arrived, so why would he expect to find anything in the forest? The answer came a moment later. If he didn't have any hope of finding something, he might as well lie down and die right here rather than continue moving forward. And appealing as he found the thought of finally joining his soulmate in whatever afterlife awaited them, he still had his revenge to claim.

How would he face her if he failed to bring the empire that killed her to justice?'

After a trudge of he knew not how long, Samaritan stood before the edge of the forest. He nearly laughed. The trees were made of metal. Some kind of black steel. He'd find nothing living in this place.

He slumped to the ground and sat with his back to the tree. Touching it pained his head, but not so much that he cared to move. In fact, he never wanted to move again. Let it all end here. He didn't care anymore.

Semiconscious, he heard the shuffling of footsteps. Probably hallucinating. He didn't bother opening his eyes to find out for sure.

"I thought more came through the bile portal," a gravelly, barely human voice said in nearly unintelligible Imperial.

"They did. According to the runes, there were five," said a similar but still distinguishably different voice.

"Then where are the rest of them?" the first voice asked.

"I haven't the slightest idea."

"Useless. This one appears still functional. Bring him and we'll see what the overmage has to say."

Samaritan found himself hoisted over a far-too-hard shoulder like a sack of potatoes. His captors, rescuers—he didn't know exactly how to categorize the strangers—carried him off into the night to meet someone called the overmage. He'd never heard that title before, but for some reason it made him think of the archbishop. Maybe these were cultists. If so, they might help him and even better have a way to contact their mistress.

With that hope firmly in mind, he finally opened his eyes. He saw nothing save the black earth and a pair of legs that appeared to be made of black iron, just like everything else in this miserable area. Cultists made of metal seemed unlikely. Certainly he would have heard of them should such an outrageous group exist.

No, he feared whoever had found him weren't allies. Samaritan knew The One God was a lie, but he was starting to wonder if the stories about Hell were based at least in part on reality. Because if this land wasn't in Hell, he feared he may have ended up somewhere even worse.

CHAPTER 9

Fane appeared in a moonlit clearing at the edge of a forest. Had she the time, Fane would have paused to enjoy the beautiful setting. It pleased her aesthetic sense far better than Beastmaster's dreary tunnels. But she didn't have time. There was power to be seized and that took precedence over everything else.

Her overseer stood about ten feet away, head lowered and silent. She shot the demon a hard look, but since it had claimed the fortress, more or less, Fane decided to refrain from criticizing.

"Tell me everything," she said.

The overseer did so. From the sound of it, the humans had learned to deal with her bile zombies. That didn't surprise her. The vermin were surprisingly adaptable; even limited to alchemy, they found a path forward. Sometimes Fane looked back at how weak she'd been before her transformation and shuddered.

On the plus side, having the overseer's magic on hand increased her minions' adaptability. That also went according to her plans. Unfortunately, she didn't have enough overseers to send one on every mission. Even worse, she lacked the power to summon and bind any more.

When the overseer finished Fane said, "So the survivors are trapped in the fortress basement and as far as you can tell they remain unharmed by the corruption that destroyed the bile beast."

"Yes, Mistress. It makes no sense to me. Given how much corruption fills the air of the basement, they should have died in minutes, yet I can still sense their undiminished life forces."

The situation made no sense to Fane either, but there was one more matter to consider before focusing on the source of corruption. "You're certain none of them escaped?"

The overseer's melted forehead crinkled. "None escaped past me. And no messenger birds were sent. Beyond that I can't say with absolute certainty."

She wanted more certainty. If it took some time to unravel this mystery, she preferred not to have to do it while dealing with an army. Powerful though she was, even Fane had her limits and they were far less impressive than Amet Sur's.

"We'll make sure." Fane pulled a pinky-sized vial of Black Bile out of her satchel and squeezed.

The vial shattered and the bile dissolved as she drained its power to activate a spell. Corrupt ether swirled and a hand-sized portal to Astaroth's hell opened. Her magic reached out and seized a corpse raven, yanking it through the nearly too small portal. She grabbed it by both legs and held it upside down like a chicken awaiting slaughter.

The huge black bird glared at her with glowing red eyes.

Fane glared back. The trick when dominating a demon-infused undead was to show them no fear. To start at least. Next she gathered ether around her body and let it radiate out in a show of power.

She used every bit she could muster and the raven quickly looked away. Good. Fane released the magic immediately.

Channeling that much ether for more than a few seconds would leave even her exhausted.

"What do you wish of me?" the raven asked. It never ceased to amaze her that such an inhuman form could speak such clear sentences.

"I want you to scout the area, say ten miles in every direction. If you find any humans, kill them. Return to me when you're finished."

"And if I find nothing?" the raven asked.

Fane shrugged. "That would be the ideal result. I don't care if you find something or not as long as anything you do find dies. Clear?"

"Perfectly."

"Good." Fane flicked her wrist and sent the raven flying into the sky.

"Think it will find anything?" the overseer asked.

"Probably not, but I didn't accomplish all I have by being reckless. Now, show me what you found."

The overseer turned without a word and strode toward the fortress. Fane followed a step behind, eager to see what awaited her.

When they reached the fortress wall, she could already sense the power underneath. In her hundreds of years of life, she'd never felt anything like it. The power seethed and roiled like a dark whirlpool. Even from a distance it felt like it wanted to suck her in.

Fane shivered with pleasure. Even if this wasn't the ultimate power she sought, when she mastered it, her might would increase tremendously. Maybe even enough to locate the sleeping dragon on her own.

"Mistress?" The overseer looked back from inside the gate.

Fane hadn't even realized she'd stopped to revel in the corruption. "I'm fine. Keep going."

He nodded and resumed his trudging pace through the

ruined keep door, down halls that looked like a tornado had hit them, and finally stopping just within sight of an open door with a set of stairs beyond it.

"The bile beast tried to descend to kill the humans below and exploded. I couldn't really tell how or why it happened. One second the undead appeared fine and the next, boom. I deemed it wise to get no closer."

She wanted to sneer and call the overseer a coward, but up close she had to admit that it had a point. When she first spotted the power source, she'd imagined finding a new bile pit or something similar, but this...

Fane shook her head. Lord Sur would know what to make of it, she felt certain, but she was at a loss. Maybe if she moved a little closer, she'd get an idea of how it destroyed the bile beast.

Steeling herself, she wove the most powerful ethereal shield possible around her body and took a step.

It felt like her body weighed ten times its true weight as some force strove to keep her from getting closer.

Her shield buckled and she leapt back an instant before it shattered.

Standing beside the overseer, she felt perfectly normal. This spot had to be right at the edge of the safe zone. Good to know that at least.

"What do you make of it?" the overseer asked.

"I wish I knew," Fane said before she could think better of it. "I can certainly see why the bile beast was destroyed. If I tried to rush in without any precautions, I likely would have suffered the same fate. As it was, my most powerful shield lasted only seconds. What I can't understand is why the humans are unaffected. I can still sense them down there and as far as I can tell they are alive and unharmed."

"That struck me as well. Do you think because we are undead and they are mortal has anything to do with it?"

"It must, but I would've thought the opposite would happen.

We should be unharmed and they should be dead." Fane shook her head. Talking wouldn't do any good. "I'm going to take a look in spirit form. Hopefully that will be enough to keep me safe. Protect my body until I return."

Fane sat, centered herself mentally, and freed her spirit from her body. Without her eyes in the way, the corruption looked even more intimidating. In all her time as Lord Sur's apprentice, she'd never seen anything like this. It looked like a vortex of corruption with the widest part of its mouth just feet in front of her.

Her spirit drifted closer and immediately the vortex tried to suck her in.

Fane fought with all her might and even then barely pulled free in time. She entered her body and opened her eyes. Her hands trembled and she kept them hidden until they stopped. Her failure already showed her weakness to an unacceptable degree. If the overseer saw her trembling hands he might get rebellious ideas and Fane had no desire to destroy a still-useful servant.

"What did you see, Mistress?"

"Nothing good. Stay here and keep watch. Should any of the humans emerge, kill them, but don't destroy the bodies. I want to see what, if anything, the corruption has done to them. I'm going for a walk."

Fane left her minion on guard duty and retraced her steps down the smashed corridor and outside. When she'd left the fortress a safe distance behind, she took a deep breath of cool night air and smiled. Even though she didn't actually need to breathe, something about the act of inhaling soothed her. Probably just a leftover from her time as a mortal.

The irony that she'd probably have no trouble walking right up to the source of corruption were she still human didn't escape Fane. Nor did it please her. In fact, the idea that her immortal body might be a hindrance rather than a help enraged her. She believed she'd left her weakness behind, and now this.

She thought back to one of Lord Sur's last lessons before she made the transformation. "Nothing is perfect," he'd said. "You do the best you can with what you have and learn to work around the deficiencies."

Fane had nearly laughed but didn't dare disrespect her master so. The idea that an arcane lord had any weaknesses struck her as hilarious. Lord Sur was closer to a god than a man.

But he also wasn't here to help her. She had to claim the power on her own. She pursed her lips. She had one option. Much as she hated it, Beastmaster might be able to go where someone like her couldn't. Calling him in to do what she couldn't felt like a failure and Fane had no doubt Beastmaster would find some way to let her know, some subtle dig that she'd be forced to ignore, at least for the moment.

She closed her eyes and focused. "Beastmaster."

A minute or so later his psychic presence appeared. "That was fast. Everything okay?"

"No." Fane described what she'd found. "Whatever sort of magic protects the power source, it destroys undead but seems to leave normal humans unharmed. I need you to come here and find a way to turn it off at the source."

"Um, I'm about as far from a normal human as you are. Are you sure the wards will let me pass?"

"At this point I'm not sure of anything. I know you're not undead and hopefully that will be enough. Come here and we'll find out."

"Okay. I'll bring one of my pets with me. If she can get through, I'll give it a shot. Oh, I gave your human a cure all. He should be back to normal in three days."

"That's fine." Fane's jaw clenched and she forced herself to relax. "Just hurry."

Ten minutes later Beastmaster appeared in a flash of ether.

He smiled at her then glanced toward the fortress. "Wow, that sure is a lot of corruption. It's weird that normal humans aren't affected by it. Shall we go have a look?"

"Yes, let's." She turned and stalked back toward the fortress. Whatever was in there better be worth all this fuss.

CHAPTER 10

Joran dipped a handful of water out of the mithril-infused pond and splashed his face. He didn't know what to make of Bahesti and his offer of help. A thousand years or so stuck in a metal body, unable to sleep, eat, or do any other sort of normal human activity might make him eager to die as well. Add to that the fact that he might once have been able to use magic and now could only see the ether and not touch it…

He stood and turned to find his companions seated in a circle waiting for him. They all looked expectantly up at him as if he'd deliver some genius solution to their problem. Pity for them all that he didn't have such a solution tucked up his sleeve. In truth, he had no idea if Bahesti actually knew anything useful or if he was a mad construct spouting fiction. Some of what he said agreed with the ancient histories Joran had read, but his knowledge was so fragmentary that it meant nothing that some matched.

Joran sat beside Mia and facing Grub and Stoneheart. "Well, you all heard what he said. What are your thoughts?"

When no one spoke, he looked at Grub and raised an eyebrow. "Anything?"

"I hate to trust anyone or anything associated with our former masters, but as you said earlier, without some sort of guide, we're liable to end up lost and dead in short order. As long as Bahesti plays it straight with us, I think we have few options."

Joran nodded and turned to Stoneheart. "Centurion?"

Stoneheart's face twisted like he'd eaten something bitter, but he said, "I agree with Grub. We work with the cursed metal man, watch him closely, and if he betrays us, give him the death he so eagerly seeks."

"No, that's the one thing we can't do," Joran said. "Whatever else happens, we must make it clear that we won't grant his wish if he betrays us. We need some other way to punish him for betrayal."

"What if I cut off his arms and legs?" Mia asked. "He'd still be alive but in worse shape than he is now."

"That's not a terrible idea. No need to antagonize him by making threats, but if it becomes necessary, I'll be counting on you to do the job. Maybe start with just his arms as a warning."

The dwarves stared at them, clearly aghast.

"What?" Joran asked. "As far as I can tell, Bahesti isn't really alive. His body is a shell for his intellect. I assume he has some kind of core where that intellect lives, probably his head or heart. The rest of him is just unfeeling metal. I'm surprised you'd care what happens to one of the people that tormented your ancestors."

"It's less that I care about Bahesti," Stoneheart said, "than it is that hearing you talk about cutting someone's arms off so casually is a shock."

That made a certain amount of sense. "Don't worry. If he was an actual living, breathing person likely to bleed to death should he lose an arm, I wouldn't be so casual. In fact, I

72

wouldn't even consider it. The problem we face is that the threat of death, in this case at least, is no threat at all. That leaves us in a difficult spot. With any luck this won't even become an issue, but I wanted to discuss our options before it did."

"Understood, Lord Den Cade," Stoneheart said.

Grub stayed silent, but voiced no more concerns.

"Good. I'll take first watch. Then Stoneheart, Grub, and Mia. Try to get some rest. I suspect we're going to have a busy day tomorrow."

———

Samaritan didn't know how long he'd been bouncing along on the metal man's shoulder, but his stomach hurt and he suspected a shoulder-sized bruise would be appearing tomorrow. Assuming, of course, that he had a tomorrow. That struck him as a rather large assumption at the moment.

He opened his eyes to find his captor walking on a path made of smoothed black dirt. They must be approaching something like civilization. Probably the home of the overmage they mentioned. He closed his eyes again to better sell the lie that he was unconscious. There seemed little point in pretending, but he figured better to speak first with the leader rather than the minions.

At last, the person carrying him stopped. Samaritan had a second to brace himself before getting unceremoniously dumped on a hard stone table.

He groaned like that was what woke him up and opened his eyes. A black iron face devoid of expression looked back at him. The person, or whatever, had fine features, like they'd been carved by a master sculptor. The flat, black eyes gave no hint of what he thought.

"Where am I?" Samaritan asked.

"You are in the Black Iron Empire and in the presence of the last overmage," the stranger said. "You should be honored."

He added that last bit seemingly just in case Samaritan didn't realize how he'd been honored. Samaritan started to sit up but a powerful hand forced him back down hard enough that his head bounced off the table.

"Please don't move around," the overmage said. "My followers are a bit overprotective. Perfectly understandable when you realize I'm the last leader of the empire. They would all be lost without me."

Samaritan had serious doubts about that, but since he had no desire to get his head bounced off the table again, he nodded. "My name is Samaritan. I was near a bile pit a few days north of Dwarfhome when something happened. The next thing I know I found myself standing on an island devoid of life. That small patch of blackened earth held nothing resembling civilization, so I went looking for some. Your followers must have found me after I passed out from exhaustion and dehydration. Do you have anything safe to drink?"

"We do not require food or drink, but I believe something can be found." The overmage snapped his fingers, making a discordant clang, and the sound of retreating footsteps followed. "Your drink will be brought. While we wait, tell me where the others that came with you have gone. The runes indicate four more came through the portal."

"I don't know where the others went and I have no great desire to find out. I barely escaped with my life the first time. A second encounter may not end as well."

"So they are your enemies. That makes more sense. My first thought was that you had split up to search a larger area, but that would have required a way for you to communicate. Not to mention four going one way and a single person another makes no sense."

Samaritan made no comment. If the overmage was supposed

to be some great leader, then he'd hate to see the followers' levels of intelligence. "How did a bile pit bring me here anyway?"

"What you found wasn't a bile pit, it was a bile portal. We designed them to use the concentrated magic of the Black Bile to create a portal that would transport everyone in the portal chamber to a predetermined location. You were fortunate that the location where you arrived still existed. Others have been completely destroyed."

Samaritan swallowed. "What would have happened if I ended up at one of those?"

"I'm not certain. Either the magic would have failed altogether or you would have appeared in the correct spot and likely fallen to your death on the broken rocks below. Since no one has ever appeared at any of those places, I can't say for sure."

More clanking footsteps preceded the overmage saying, "Your drink is here. You have my permission to sit up."

Samaritan did so with considerable relief. He found himself seated on a table made of black iron about ten strides from an equally black tower lacking its upper floors. One metal man stood right beside the table while a second carrying a wine bottle approached from the direction of the tower.

The overmage took the bottle from his servant and handed it to Samaritan. "We have no water, but the tower wine cellar is well stocked. Food, alas, is harder to come by."

Samaritan took the bottle, put the cork between his teeth, and yanked it out. The moisture felt wonderful sliding down his throat even if it did taste like vinegar. He took two more long pulls before replacing the cork. He didn't want to get drunk while dealing with this possibly insane man.

"Feel better?" the overmage asked.

"Much, thank you."

"Excellent. Now to business. What are your intentions in my empire?"

Samaritan considered his answer carefully. Given his condition and weapons, he had no hope of defeating or even escaping his rescuers, or maybe captors would be a better description. Either way, he was completely at their mercy.

"That's a difficult question to answer. Since I had no idea I'd end up here, naturally I had no plans for when I arrived. That said, finding a way home would be at the top of my list. An ally of mine is also interested in visiting the capital of your empire. If I had some way to contact her, I could introduce you."

"I appreciate your honesty. Getting you home will be difficult. There are still functioning bile portals, but I control none of them. I can point you in the correct direction, but that's it. Tell me more about your ally and what she wants here."

"The archbishop—that's what she calls herself—is interested in the giant beasts you made, specifically the techniques you used to do so. She wishes to copy the process to create weapons of her own. There are also rumors of an even more powerful creature whose power the empire tapped. We both hoped to wake that power and use it to destroy our enemies."

The overmage chuckled. "Your ally is a fool."

Samaritan winced. Hopefully he wouldn't say that to the archbishop's face. Metal man or not, he'd likely end up a puddle of slag.

"The giant beasts you mentioned were one of our greatest failures. Tremendous resources were expended to create them only to watch the cursed things run amok destroying the labs that created them. More resources were wasted subduing them and putting them into hiding."

"If they were such failures, why not kill them and be done with it?"

"The Council declared that it would be an even greater waste to destroy them. We might find some way to control the beasts in the future and if we did, we could wake them again."

"I take it you didn't find a way."

The overmage's voice held a hint of humor when he said, "No. Instead we found the creature you and your ally seek. Look around and understand what you hope to find. The dragon—"

"Wait a moment." Samaritan stared and tried to wrap his mind around that. "A dragon. That's the empire's ultimate weapon?"

"Weapon? You misunderstand. We don't and never did control the dragon. We didn't even know there was a dragon until we woke it accidentally while seeking the source of Black Bile. The beast did not appreciate our uninvited intrusion into its lair. It smashed our continent to pieces and transformed what remained into black iron. Even the colonies across the sea sustained damage, though the dragon did show some mercy by only transforming this continent."

Samaritan's mind raced. If he found the dragon and somehow convinced it that the Tiberian Empire sent him to wake it, the beast might do to them what it did to the Black Iron Empire. What a glorious revenge that would be. To see all those that betrayed his faith and killed his soulmate laid to waste or transformed into living metal.

"As for finding the capital," the overmage went on, seeming unaware of Samaritan's drifting thoughts. "The archbishop is going to be disappointed. The dragon obliterated it before sinking the ashes to the bottom of the ocean. There is nothing left to find."

"You're right, she certainly won't like that. Is there some-where else we might find the knowledge we seek?"

"You still wish to find the dragon after everything I just told you?" The overmage cocked his head as if having trouble under-standing.

Samaritan wasn't surprised by that. Anyone else would certainly be turned aside by that story, but for him, nothing could be more perfect. The dragon represented the culmination of everything he sought. It would be the perfect instrument for his revenge.

"I do, now more than ever. Will you help me?"

"As it happens, I too wish to wake the dragon again, though for reasons of my own. Perhaps together we can succeed where I have failed."

Samaritan grinned and held out his hand. He didn't care in the least why the overmage wanted to wake the dragon. As long as it destroyed the Tiberian Empire, nothing else mattered. "Agreed."

The overmage shook, the black iron of his hand as cold and unyielding as the archbishop's had been when he agreed to work with her. Would she be upset that he found a new partner? After a moment's consideration he decided it didn't matter as she was far from here and in no position to stop him in any case.

"You are tired," the overmage said. "Drink and rest. We will set out in the morning."

"Very well, but can I ask your name? Calling you Overmage is a bit odd."

"Odd or not, it will have to do. I may have had another name once, but if I did, I no longer remember what it was. Overmage is the only name that means anything to me now."

Samaritan certainly couldn't comment on anyone's choice of names given his own preference. "As you wish, Overmage. Is there anywhere on our journey where we might find food?"

Overmage shrugged. "Doubtful, but we can look in the ruins we'll pass. Rest now. I must return and check the runes."

Samaritan nodded and pulled the cork out of his wine bottle. He'd drink a toast to the death of his enemies. May they all rot in whatever hell the dragon sent them to.

CHAPTER 11

Gaius forced himself not to run through the forest. He had a long ways to go to reach civilization, much less the capital. At least once he found a village, he'd be able to requisition a horse, hopefully a decent one and not a farmer's draft horse. That should speed his journey considerably. At the bigger towns he'd find churches, most of which would have small stables allowing him to change mounts every few days. If The One God smiled on him, he should reach Tiber in a month.

His jaw clenched and once again he forced himself to relax. He needed to get there faster. Heaven knew what the wizard controlling that monster might do if he got the demon artifact. It could be a disaster beyond anything the empire had ever experienced. Even worse, His Imperial Majesty might blame the church for letting it fall into the hands of an enemy.

He ducked a branch and leapt a jutting boulder. One thing at a time. First a town, then a horse. Worry about the rest later.

He kept his course mostly west and a little south. Every White Knight had to memorize the land between the fortress and the capital. Gaius had thought it a foolish waste of time when Florens ordered him to do so then quizzed him until he was satisfied that Gaius had the knowledge firmly in his mind.

Now Gaius sent a silent prayer of thanks to his superior. Those lessons would end up saving his life.

A chill ran down his spine and every instinct screamed *duck*.

Gaius didn't question that feeling. He hit the dirt just as something flew through the space he just vacated. It had to be some kind of large bird, but he'd never heard of a bird that would attack humans. At least not healthy, running humans.

He scrambled to his feet and ripped his sword from its sheath. Whatever had happened, he didn't have time to fool around. He had to deal with the creature sooner rather than later.

Putting his back to a tree, Gaius studied the gaps in the branches. It had to be there somewhere.

A rustle of wings warned him.

He swung and struck something a heavy blow. He caught a glimpse of black feathers as a giant bird flapped once, righted itself, and soared out of sight into the canopy.

Gaius checked the edge of his sword. No blood despite making solid contact. That confirmed his fear that he'd run into some sort of supernatural creature.

"Surrender, human," a voice called from the treetops. "And I'll make your death painless."

"You don't make a very compelling argument." Gaius shrugged out of his pack. "I have no quarrel with you. Could you not just let me go on my way?"

"My mistress would be most displeased should I do such a thing and she is not the sort one displeases lightly."

Gaius rummaged through the pack until he found the vial he wanted. The alchemists put one in every survival pack. The thick, silver liquid was supposed to make your sword sharper and stronger than naked imperial steel. Gaius had no idea if it would be enough to defeat the bird monster, but he had no other options save dying. He used half the vial to cover both edges.

"Then it seems we have no choice but to fight." Gaius listened hard, trying to figure out where the bird was based on its reply.

"Yes." The answer came from directly behind him.

The bird creature loosed a shrill caw and snapped its wings.

Gaius spun and swung.

Pain ran down his right arm even as he felt the edge of his sword bite deep into the monster's flesh.

The bird hit the ground, both legs severed and its belly feathers shaved off. Gaius checked his arm and found blood running from a deep gash in his shoulder. He winced, but at least it hadn't been his throat that got cut.

Now that he finally got a good look at the thing, he decided it was a crow, the biggest one he'd ever seen. Of course, had he doubted its unnatural origin, the glowing red eyes combined with the fact that it still lived with no legs would have tipped him off to his error.

"Well struck," the crow said.

It flopped around, prompting Gaius to put his sword on its breast. "Tell me about your mistress."

The crow laughed, a surprisingly human sound. "She is the most powerful wizard on your world. Had she truly believed a knight had escaped, she would have summoned something far stronger than I to hunt you down. Good fortune walks with you, young knight."

Gaius shook his head. "Fortune didn't save me, The One God's blessing did. You were an honorable opponent. Take pride in that when you return to whatever hell spat you out."

The crow laughed again. "Honor has no place in Astaroth's hell. Only power and victory matter and I have little of the first and none of the second."

"Then take my pity back with you." Gaius pressed down,

driving the tip of his sword through the crow's breast, not stopping until it hit dirt.

The creature dissolved into a black mist before vanishing. Only the lingering odor of brimstone remained behind.

Gaius never thought he'd meet an actual demon, much less one so well spoken and with manners. The more he saw and learned, the less everything he thought he knew made sense.

He returned the partially used vial to his pack and collected the tin of crimson paste. A thick dollop of troll's blood ointment eased the pain of his wound, though it failed to fully wash it away. That said something about the crow's power, despite what it thought. An ordinary wound of similar depth would have been fully healed by the ointment.

No time to puzzle over it now. He put his pack back together and slung it over his left shoulder. He had a long ways to go and if another magical enemy presented itself, he'd have only one chance to defeat it. The effects of the silver oil had already faded.

Sheathing his sword, he set out. He sent a prayer to The One God that the rest of his journey might be less eventful.

———

A s Beastmaster walked down the ruined hall beside Fane, the oppressive nature of the corruption grew ever clearer. He felt it in his bones, and his stomach clenched and twisted. Assuming she wasn't telling him a story, and Fane wasn't exactly known for her sense of humor, then normal humans had not only come down this corridor on a regular basis, but they actually lived here without issue. That seemed impossible.

He pulled the three-eyed squirrel he'd brought with him to test the danger partway out of a pocket and found her twitching more than usual, but otherwise calm. If she felt anything like what he did, she should be going berserk. A thread of ether connected their minds. She felt a little uncomfortable and would have preferred to leave, but otherwise he sensed no hesitation in her mind.

He let her fall back out of sight. "If this gets any worse, I think I'm going to throw up."

"So it is affecting you," Fane said. "Interesting. Clearly being undead has no bearing on how the corruption acts. Though it doesn't make me feel ill, just on edge. Once we get closer the real danger begins."

"You probably don't feel sick because you haven't eaten anything in centuries. I, on the other hand, had a delicious steak for dinner. How much further?"

"Not far. Though if you're already having this much trouble, I can't imagine there's any way you'll be able to explore the source."

Beastmaster couldn't argue with that. "Maybe not directly, but if I mind link with my pet, she might be able to go in and take a look around for me. The corruption doesn't seem to bother her much."

Fane frowned. "What did you bring?"

He pulled his pet all the way out of his pocket. "A three-eyed squirrel. I made her on a whim one day. She's not really good for combat, but she is cute."

The squirrel shied away when Fane got closer. None of his pets liked her. Not that they liked any undead, but they really didn't like Fane.

"How much Black Bile did you use to make this thing?"

"A couple drops. It was just the dregs from another project. Why?"

"I wonder if the bile is the secret. I used a great deal to make my overseer and he used plenty to make the bile beast. As an undead, I'm infused with corruption which is close enough to make it seem like I was made with bile. And you work with the stuff all the time. That might be what's setting off the defenses."

Beastmaster nodded. "Makes sense, but if you're right, we've got a major problem. Everyone in the cult has either spent time around or otherwise used Black Bile at one time or another. That's going to make it hard to find someone we can send in. Not to mention that if we send in a normal cultist, the knights below will just kill them."

"All true. For now, let's focus on seeing if you can even get a glimpse of what's down there through your rat's eyes."

"Squirrel. She's a squirrel, not a rat, though they are related. Rats are much uglier." Beastmaster gave his pet a pat on the head. "She didn't mean anything by that insult. You're a good squirrel and if you make it back, I've got a nice, fresh finger for you to snack on."

"It eats meat?" Fane asked.

"Well, I did mutate her with Black Bile. For some reason she got a taste for blood after that. They all do really." Beastmaster shrugged. "One of the side effects I guess. Not a big deal since I have an easier time finding meat than acorns anyway."

They rounded a corner and found Fane's overseer waiting near a doorway. This had to be the place judging by the amount of corruption in the air. Beastmaster shivered. He really didn't want to get any closer.

"No change, Mistress," the overseer said.

"Good. Okay, Beastmaster, see what you can find."

He took a deep breath and swallowed a sigh. He set the squirrel on the floor and sent threads of ether into its tiny brain. When he closed his eyes, he suddenly found the view far lower to the ground. Controlling it like a puppet, he sent her across the floor and down the steps.

She didn't explode, though she also really didn't want to get any closer to whatever was downstairs. He didn't blame her, but they had a job to do, so he urged her on.

"What do you see?" Fane asked.

"She's still on the stairs. I'm having her go slowly so she can get used to the corruption in the air. It's already at least twice as thick as it is up here."

"That's impossible. If the trend holds, there will be nothing but corrupt ether at the bottom. Normal humans should have no hope of surviving in such an environment."

"You asked me what I saw, and that's what I see. She's almost to the bottom of the steps." Beastmaster fell silent to better focus on the connection.

His pet scurried off the bottom step and looked around a little entry area with a second door about ten feet away. Not exactly ideal. There was a little gap at the bottom, but even his pet had no hope of squeezing under it.

Maybe he could at least get a peek at what was on the other side.

At his urging, the squirrel shoved her head under the door as far as it would go. Inside, he found a big room filled with White Knights. They sat around, some eating, others drinking. One, an older fellow Beastmaster figured was in charge, paced around like a caged giant weasel. None of them looked sick or especially anxious. Bored seemed like the dominant emotion.

His view shifted and his jaw dropped when he spotted the source of the corruption.

"What is it?" Fane asked. She must have noticed his reaction.

"I'm not sure what it is," Beastmaster said. "There's a black orb as big as my head sitting on a tripod of black iron. That's the source of the corruption. There are also about thirty White Knights lounging in the room with it seeming no worse for wear."

"Show me," Fane said.

His pet squeaked and fled as one of the knights lunged toward it. Beastmaster called her back and severed the link. He opened his eyes and when the blurriness went away looked up at Fane. "They spotted her. Not that it matters since I saw everything worth seeing."

Beastmaster gathered ether and crafted an illusion of the orb and tripod. "This is what it looked like."

Fane walked all around it shaking her head. "I've never seen or read about anything like this. Can you tell what it does through the ether?"

Beastmaster shook his head then smiled as his pet climbed up his pant leg and perched on his shoulder. He dug a severed finger out of his pocket and handed it to her as promised. She started nibbling at once.

"If you're done playing with that rat, can you tell me more about the orb?"

"As far as I can see, all it does is emit corruption. If the orb has another purpose, it's not readily apparent."

Fane bared her fangs. She was getting crabby again. "It has to have another purpose."

"I don't disagree, but I still can't tell what."

"Why don't we kill the humans guarding it and send a human cultist to bring the bloody thing upstairs?" the overseer said.

Fane spun to look at him and the poor guy flinched. Beastmaster actually felt kind of bad for the demon. He considered himself more of an ally than a servant and he still got a little nervous when she glared like that.

"That's not a terr—" She put a hand to her head.

"What?" Beastmaster asked.

"Someone killed my corpse crow. An escaped White Knight no doubt. A skilled one if he managed to defeat even a weak demon. Once word gets back to Tiber, we'll have a legion bearing down on us."

Beastmaster cocked his head. "It'll take weeks for someone to reach the capital and a couple months for a legion to march out here. And even then, it's not like ordinary soldiers, no matter how many of them show up, could stop us from just leaving."

"You're right, of course. I simply dislike the idea of having to abandon such a potentially valuable artifact. As the overseer said, killing the knights and having one of our human pawns fetch the orb might be the best idea."

"Do you think so?" Beastmaster asked. "I mean, if you can't turn off whatever is making it destroy anyone filled with corruption, bringing it upstairs will only force you to move further away. I'd say your best bet is to return to your citadel and search the archives specifically for the orb. Once you have a better idea what it is and how to deal with it, moving it makes more sense."

She shot him the crabby glare, but he knew Fane well enough to recognize the lack of heat in her expression. His knees didn't even wobble.

"I hate it when you're right. Return to your workshop and get the prisoner sorted out. I'll head home and start my own research. Overseer, you will remain behind. Kill anyone that tries to escape and save the body for examination."

"Yes, Mistress."

Beastmaster headed for the door at once, throwing a little wave over his shoulder. The sooner he got home and away from Fane, the happier he'd be. Even if he did have to babysit her pet human.

CHAPTER 12

Light had just begun to color the sky bloodred when Joran sat up. That didn't shock him, yet he still found waking up in this dead land with a sky that looked ready to bleed disheartening. He'd had a fitful night's sleep despite feeling exhausted. They'd learned so much and yet he really didn't understand most of it. Making decisions with imperfect information while knowing they might decide the fate of not only the empire but the world didn't exactly lead to restful nights.

"Finally gave up?" Mia sat a little ways away from the group, the mithril sword resting on her lap as she watched the area. "If you got more than three hours' sleep last night, I'd be shocked."

"Busy mind. Anything interesting happen during your watch?"

"Not a thing. I seriously doubt there's enough life in the country to fill a dragon ship."

"Depending on what you consider Bahesti and his people, there might not be any. If you're willing to help, I'd like to conduct an experiment before we set out."

She beamed. "I'd love to. What do you want me to do?"

He stood. "Come with me."

They made the short walk over to the nearest iron tree and he pointed at a small, low-hanging branch. "Slice that off."

"Don't you think it might wake the dwarves?"

"It's almost time to get up anyway, but no, I don't think it will."

She shrugged, squared up to the branch, and swung. Just as Joran expected, the mithril blade passed through the branch silently and with no visible resistance. Unlike the Hell-forged blade back in Tiber, this metal had considerably poorer durability.

Now for phase two. "Poke the tip of your sword into it and hold it there until I tell you to take it out."

Again she obliged him without question. He dearly appreciated that as he was still trying to come up with a coherent theory and anything he said now would make little sense even to him.

A few seconds passed and a hint of black steam rose from the wood. Joran smiled as his theory was confirmed. It took most of a minute, but when he told Mia to remove her sword, the black iron had been fully transformed back into wood, ash judging from the now-white center.

"Wow." Mia smiled back at him. "We could have a fire tonight."

"Better than that, if we find any food or water, we've proven that you can purify it. That's a pretty important bit of information considering how hungry I am."

Her stomach growled in agreement. "What now?"

"Now we wake the dwarves and see what Bahesti has planned for us."

A few minutes of grumbling followed by drinking as much water as possible before filling their skins to near bursting saw Joran and his companions ready to set out. Despite the sun having fully risen, it still felt like twilight under the clouds.

Having made the trip once, Joran didn't find the second trip to Bahesti's village, if that was the correct word for it, nearly as daunting.

When they arrived amidst the broken towers and humble hovels, the two black iron golems were standing guard. They looked like the same ones that accompanied Bahesti when he first made contact with them. Of course, they might all look like that, Joran had no idea.

They stopped a few strides from the golems. Before Joran could draw a breath to shout for Bahesti, the man emerged from his hut. A wave of his hand sent the golems a few strides away.

"Welcome back, my new friends. I assume since you are here, you have decided to take me up on my offer of partnership."

"We have," Joran said. "Just so we're clear, you're offering to help us find information about the dragon's resting place as well as a bile portal that will take us somewhere safe in exchange for Mia killing you with her mithril sword."

"That is precisely the arrangement I had in mind."

"Excellent. Where do we begin?"

"The one most likely to know something about the quest to locate the source of the Black Bile would be the overmage that ruled this sector of the empire. I know where his citadel lies, but I haven't scouted it out myself, so there may be nothing left to search depending on the dragon's whim when he passed over this part of the empire."

"Sounds like a good place to start," Joran said. "We're ready when you are."

Bahesti spread his hands to the sides. "Everything I have, I carry with me at all times. I'll bring one golem to watch over the camp while you sleep. The other I'll leave here to protect those of my people too damaged to fend for themselves. Follow me. Barring any issues, we should reach the citadel in a week or so."

Joran grimaced. "Any chance we'll pass a farm or something where we might find food?"

"There are farms along the way, though I doubt you'll be able to find anything uncorrupted."

"Leave that to us," Joran said. "You find the farm and we'll make any food edible."

"As you wish. It will add no significant time to the journey in any case."

With the details sorted out, the now slightly larger group set out. Beyond the ruined city, they found the walking easy and the landscape bleak. Nothing but dead, blackened land for as far as Joran could see in every direction. Living in such a place had to be bad for your mental state. They'd only been here for a little over a day and he had already grown weary of it.

After a mile of trudging through the empty plains Joran asked, "Does it ever actually rain? The sky has been as black as the ground since we got here."

"It does rain from time to time," Bahesti said without looking back. "But if you look closer and use your magical vision, you'll see that those aren't clouds, they're a fog of corruption. I believe the dragon put them there to kill any birds that might try to return lest they lighten the atmosphere."

"Wow," Mia said. "That dragon really hated your people."

"Yes. The dragon of corruption seems to hate all life, yet the overmages still called it our world's guardian. I've spent many hours mulling over exactly what that means, but despite centuries of thinking, I've come up with no useful answers."

"Maybe if some sort of external threat were to appear, a demon invasion or something," Joran said. "The dragon would fight them off. But otherwise it might be wise to leave it in peace."

"I have no idea if the first part of your theory is true, but I can fully attest to the wisdom of leaving it in peace."

Joran smiled at Bahesti's back. He normally enjoyed a

mystery, but he preferred ones that didn't kill you if you came up with the wrong answer.

———

Samaritan sat up, head throbbing, body aching, and decided he'd survived the night. His stomach snarled at him and acid bubbled up the back of his throat. Right, a whole bottle of wine and no food didn't make for a happy body. He hadn't gotten drunk like last night since his college days. Even if it was practically vinegar, he wished Titus had been here to share the bottle. Hopefully his dear friend remained safe in Dwarfhome.

He got up off the ground and sat on the iron table where Overmage had questioned him the night before. He had next to nothing left of his alchemy supplies, but he did have a few strips of what he assumed was rat jerky provided by the dwarven rebels. Right now, even that sounded appetizing.

The jerky proved tasty if tougher than boot leather. As he worked at getting the first strip down, Samaritan looked up at the sky. Another bleak, leaden day. In this place, he expected nothing better. Granted a little sun would be nice, but it wasn't like the nonexistent plant life needed it to survive.

He had just started gnawing on his second strip of meat when Overmage emerged from his ruined tower, another corked bottle in his hand. A quick glance around revealed no sign of the two lackeys that carried him here. The other metal men's absence made him nervous. Not that he had any hope of killing them or escaping should he find himself betrayed. Probably best not to worry about it.

"Good morning," Overmage said. "I trust you slept well."

"Nothing like drinking a full bottle of wine to help you sleep. Speaking of which, this jerky is mighty dry."

"Of course." Overmage held out the bottle.

A long swig washed the last of the jerky down. This bottle actually had decent flavor, unlike the last one.

"Thank you. Whenever you're ready, I'm good to go."

"Splendid. I packed up every bottle of wine in the tower. It should be enough to last you several weeks, possibly more if you ration it. I sent my servants ahead to scout the path. While there is little enough living in this ruined country, there are a few beasts that survived the apocalypse."

Samaritan took one last swallow and corked the bottle. He didn't want his head too muddy for the journey.

"What sort of beasts?"

"Demonic ones mostly. The sort untroubled by the over-whelming corruption wielded by the dragon. We used them for various duties, primarily guarding sensitive areas and occasion-ally assassination. With the ether so twisted that it's nearly unusable, the binding spells have broken as well. They don't trouble us. Black iron flesh doesn't rend or bleed, so they have little interest in hunting my people. You may be another matter."

"Any more good news?"

"That isn't good news. My servants will do their best to drive off any beasts we encounter, but should they fail, your steel sword will be of little use against the demons."

"Was sarcasm not a thing in your empire?" Samaritan patted his sword. "I don't suppose you have anything that might be of more use?"

"Before the dragon, I was a wizard. Normal weapons were superfluous for me. Besides, that's what bodyguards are for. Much like the food you require, we may find a weapon that will be of some use on our journey, but I really don't know for sure."

Samaritan shrugged. "We'll do what we have to."

After a brief pause to collect a pack stuffed with wine bottles, the pair set off to the northwest. They walked in silence for most of an hour before the bleak landscape started to overwhelm Samaritan. He needed a distraction and he needed it now.

"Is our destination on this island?"

"No. Unfortunately, we'll need to cross a rather narrow stone bridge to reach the regional library. It's a pale imitation of the one in Iron City, but at least it isn't sitting on the bottom of the ocean. Anyway, don't worry, that's still many days away."

"I had to hopscotch across a bunch of stone pillars to reach this island. A bridge, no matter how narrow, will be an improvement."

Overmage looked back. "You haven't seen the bridge yet."

CHAPTER 13

Two days of walking across the bleak countryside felt like far longer to Joran. Only Bahesti seemed unaffected by it. No doubt nearly a thousand years of experience made it easier to tolerate. The previous night they'd sat around a campfire made of purified wood and Bahesti explained where they were going: the local overmage's citadel also held the regional library. It seemed every region in the empire had one, both for the local overmage's use as well as the many lesser wizards that populated the land. With the central library destroyed, it seemed the most likely place try.

That seemed reasonable to Joran, especially since he had no better ideas. They had five more days of walking ahead of them but at least the citadel was on this island, sparing them the need to cross any more gaps. He shuddered at the memory of jumping from pillar to pillar. If he never had to perform that stunt again, it would suit him perfectly well.

"Look," Mia said, pulling him out of his thoughts.

Joran turned to look where she pointed and found the roof of what had to be a barn jutting up in the distance. Of course, like everything else, it appeared to be made of black iron. The barn interested him a good deal less than the possibility of animals they could turn back into flesh and eat. His stomach was convinced he'd forgotten all about it and it made its displeasure known at regular intervals.

"Dairy farms, I believe," Bahesti said. "Do you wish to take a look?"

The possibility of beef made Joran's mouth water. "I believe we would."

They shifted course a fraction and an hour later found themselves standing a few feet away from a barn not much smaller than the mansion where Joran grew up. He suspected it would have held hundreds of cows at once. He'd never read about anything this scale in the empire. The biggest farm he knew about had eighty head of dairy cattle and the guy's neighbors all thought he'd lost his mind.

Mia's sword cleared its sheath. "Where's the door?"

They walked around the corner and found an open door. Inside were scores of milking stalls, most of them with black iron cows standing unmoving inside. Even the straw and fodder had been transformed. A dozen of the iron cows had workers seated beside them, their bodies appearing carved of obsidian.

"How come some people ended up still sort of alive and others ended up like these poor bastards?" Grub asked.

Joran had been thinking the same thing and so didn't chastise him.

Bahesti just shrugged. "I haven't the least idea. Unfortunately, you'll find far more like these than you will the 'still vaguely living' like me."

"Unfortunate for whom?" Joran asked.

"That depends entirely on your point of view."

Joran smiled without humor and walked over to the nearest cow. It reached all the way to his shoulder. They didn't need five hundred pounds of meat and had no time to dry a whole cow. Luckily Joran did have some preservative in his kit.

"Mia, please slice off a rear quarter and start the purification process. Grub, Stoneheart, once she's finished, regular blades will cut the meat with no issue. I'll need you two to slice it into strips."

Mia got right to work but Grub said, "What about you?"

"I'll prepare the preservation powder. We'll aim for around fifty pounds of meat. That should last us a good month, assuming we can find water to go with it."

"Never thought I'd say this," Stoneheart said. "But some vegetables would be nice."

Joran agreed wholeheartedly. "If this is the barn, there has to be a bunkhouse or something where the workers lived. Maybe we can find something there."

"I can go with you while your companions prepare the meat," Bahesti said.

"Wait for me," Mia said. "I won't be long."

She had a chunk of haunch on the floor and her sword thrust six inches into it.

"I'm just going outside for a look," Joran said. "I won't move beyond our link."

She didn't look pleased at the prospect of him even moving out of her sight, but at last she nodded.

Joran and Bahesti went back outside and walked around the barn. When they rounded the end, the bunkhouse—or at least that's what Joran assumed it was—waited twenty yards away. It measured about a tenth the size of the barn. Hopefully they'd have everything the hungry group needed.

"Your lady friend is quite protective," Bahesti said.

"Mia's my soulmate and we've had some adventures lately that occasionally left me in rough shape. I can't argue with her protective instincts."

"You're very fortunate. I longed to find my own soulmate. Now I wonder if I even have a soul to bond."

Joran had no idea and less inclination to offer empty reassurance. "How much of this island have you explored?"

"Most of it. I need about five days to cross it, but bear in mind that I walked nonstop. A flesh-and-blood human would probably need at least twice that. The number of... survivors"—he said that last word as if uncertain it was the right one—"were depressingly few. And the ones actually in their right mind were fewer yet. In fact, I gathered everyone willing to join me at my village. You saw our numbers and they were the best of the lot. Others wander the land like zombies, seemingly totally unaware of anything around them. Horrendously sad. I doubt the dragon could have come up with a crueler punishment."

"That was likely the idea." Joran frowned. "Something's coming."

"Something" turned out to be the guardian golem Bahesti brought with him. Joran had been wondering where it was, but assumed it wouldn't be far off.

"I sent it to scout the area," Bahesti said as if reading his mind. "Unlike a typical golem, these have a rudimentary intelligence."

Joran sensed Mia approaching a moment before the golem reached them. "Excellent timing."

"What's going on?"

"We'll find out shortly."

"Report," Bahesti said to the golem.

The construct proceeded to make a number of hand gestures, altering the number of fingers it held up as well as their orientation. The strange display meant nothing to Joran, but Bahesti nodded along as if he understood everything perfectly well.

When the golem went still Bahesti said, "We have the poor fortune to have drawn the notice of the local predators, a pack of hyenataurs."

"A pack of what?" Mia asked.

"Hyenataurs. Half humanoid, half hyena, and all demon." Bahesti shook his head. "The pack must have crossed over from one of the other islands as I didn't encounter them during any of my earlier explorations. However they got here, we need to fall back to the barn. One good thing about iron walls: they provide a good defensive position. They'll have to come at us through the door."

As the three of them plus the golem fell back Joran said, "I have some alchemist's fire and poison in my kit."

"Don't waste it. The fire might hurt them, but they drink poison like it's water. No, this fight is going to fall to Lady Mia. If we're lucky, the sight of a mithril sword might be enough to get them to flee."

A horrid, high-pitched giggle filled the air. Joran doubted he'd ever heard such an insane, evil sound in his life.

"I hope they don't run," he said. "I'd rather deal with them here, when we have an advantage, than out on the open plains where they can surround us."

"You'll likely get your wish. Hyenataurs are as stupid as they are vicious. The wizards always kept them on a tight leash when they summoned them."

They reached the doors and ducked inside. Joran closed one side and found a lock to hold it shut. The other he left open just enough to let Mia stand inside and swing freely.

Three, four-legged shapes appeared on the horizon. They carried long weapons, spears or polearms most likely. The demons had red skin on their humanoid half and matching shaggy fur on their animal half. Short, sharp horns like a goat's jutted from their brows. Their eyes glowed crimson and needle-sharp teeth filled their mouths.

"What's going on?" Stoneheart asked.

"Trouble coming," Joran said. "Keep working on the meat. Grub, do you know any magic useful against demons?"

"My spells might hurt them, but I'm not nearly strong enough to kill even a weak demon."

"Do what you can if Mia gets in trouble, but otherwise stay out of it. Bahesti, have your golem hold the door partway shut. We don't want more than one of the things getting inside at once."

Bahesti gave the order and the golem braced itself behind the door.

"Is there anything I can do to help you?" Joran asked Mia.

"No. Keep your distance so I can focus on the fight."

"I won't say be careful since I know it's impossible, but please take care of yourself."

She grinned. "Don't worry, this is something I can do. I'm not especially good at thinking through problems, but I can cut them down with no problem."

Joran smiled back before moving to stand near Stoneheart. He noted absently that the dwarves had a fair pile of beef strips ready for treating. Assuming they lived through the next few minutes, food, at least, wouldn't be an issue for some time.

And he felt certain they would survive. Mia would see to that.

———

Mia stood in the barn door and waited for the monsters to approach. The mithril sword felt light in her hand, as if eager to cut demon flesh. Joran would probably say that was silly. That she was projecting her own feelings into her weapon.

And maybe she was. Since they arrived in this forsaken country, she'd felt useless. As a warrior, her talents lay in direct confrontations with the enemy. For a long time, she'd assumed this dead land held no living residents.

Did demons actually count as living? Mia didn't know and it probably didn't matter anyway.

The creatures outside—what did Bahesti call them... hyenataurs—loosed another round of mad cackles. The sound sent a chill up her back. They probably wanted to scare their prey into making a foolish decision. Certainly that noise would scare most people. Mia, having faced down a giant serpent that could have swallowed the demons whole, didn't scare so easily.

She caught a flash of movement as they ran past the open door, just a red blur followed by the stink of brimstone, then the demons were past.

From behind her Bahesti said, "Hyenataurs like to play with their food."

Mia's grip tightened on her sword. "I am no one's food. And if they try and play with me, I'll make them regret their arrogance."

She caught the thump of approaching paws a moment before a leaf-shaped spearhead came darting in toward her head.

The mithril sword snapped up, slicing the first three feet off, and sending the black iron spearhead crashing to the floor. The rest of the spear shaft withdrew and the demons ran off again.

One weapon down.

She kicked the ruined spear tip out of the way, never taking her gaze off the doorway. "You didn't mention they were cowards."

"They're demons," Bahesti said. "They torture and murder anything weaker than them and cower before anything stronger. Right now, they're trying to figure out which category you fit into. Though since you're human, that pretty much automatically puts you into column one."

The conversation ended when the hyenataurs came charging in again. This time all three of them raced right at the door at once. The one whose spear she destroyed had ugly red flames dancing around his hands.

If that thing could throw fire, this fight wasn't going to last long.

At ten yards it still hadn't cast a spell.

At five yards she braced herself as the center demon leveled its spear right at her heart.

Mia twisted her wrists and smashed the spear aside with the flat of the blade.

It drove into the closed door, rattling it in the frame.

She lunged forward and slashed.

The mithril blade took the demon's left hand at the wrist.

It howled in pain and pulled back.

The first one she disarmed threw a flaming punch at her head.

Her sword flicked up and out, splitting its fist in half along with most of its forearm.

That was enough for round two. All three demons rushed away. The severed hand steamed as it slowly melted into a puddle of black goo that got absorbed into the dirt.

"How are we doing?" Joran asked from behind her.

"They're bleeding and I'm not, so I'm calling that a win for us."

"Ha! Never doubted you for a second." She knew through their link that he was telling the truth and she loved him for it.

"I must admit I'm impressed as well," Bahesti said. "Most humans don't fare nearly as well against demons, even relatively weak ones like the hyenataurs. No doubt a mithril sword makes a huge difference. Still, your courage is most impressive."

Somehow Mia believed him as well, though the way he said it made his compliment sound sarcastic. Probably just his way of speaking. She didn't know him well enough to say for sure one way or the other.

"Can you tell where they went?" Joran asked.

Mia looked left and right, but didn't dare leave her post at the door. "I can't see them from here and I can't hear their footsteps. Maybe they fled. Two of them are hurt pretty bad."

"Not a chance," Bahesti said. "Once you wounded them, this became a personal fight. They won't run. They'll kill us or we'll kill them. There's no middle ground."

A horrendous crash from the rear of the barn made Mia jump. She risked a glance.

The iron boards gave way under the blows of a pair of flaming paws. Looked like two of the demons had circled around and were making their own entrance. If she went to deal with them, the third would doubtless attack the door.

She ground her teeth in frustration, but the relentless pounding on the rear wall made it clear that she had little time to waste.

"Push the door shut and have your golem hold it," Mia said.

Bahesti gave the order without comment and a moment later the door slammed shut.

"I can delay one of them for a minute or two," Grub said.

Mia let out a breath of relief. "Thanks."

With the door as protected as she could make it, Mia ran for the rear wall.

The demons had nearly broken through when she arrived. The two injured ones had attacked the back wall with their beast parts to make up for their wounded humanoid bodies. She'd never fought anything so tough that the loss of a limb wouldn't balk it. Demons truly were terrifying creatures.

Terrifying or not, her sword still hurt them. And if she could hurt them, then she could kill them, assuming she landed a blow somewhere vital.

Time to find out.

She lunged at the one-armed demon an instant before it struck the wall.

With all of its momentum coming forward, it had no hope of dodging.

Mia's sword ran it through up to the hilt.

She ripped it back and to the side, cutting the demon nearly in half.

It reached out with its good hand and grabbed her wrist in a crushing grasp.

Even worse, its partner chose that moment to rear back and swing its flaming paws at her chest.

Before it had a chance to strike, a glass vial exploded against its side and thick brown ooze stuck it to the wall.

The heat from its flailing legs scorched her face, but nothing worse.

The somehow still alive if nearly halved demon finally released her.

Mia spun and swung, sending the stuck demon's head flying.

She glanced back at Joran and he gave her a thumbs-up.

The third demon chose that moment to attack.

It smashed through the partial opening its now-dead companions had made and slammed into Mia, sending her flying.

She landed hard, flat on her back, the air rushing out of her in a burst. The mithril sword slid about ten feet away.

The demon roared and spun, spear leveled at her chest.

It charged.

Mia scrambled back, gasping for breath, desperate to reach her sword.

Five feet from her, a blast of lightning struck the demon, drawing a pained shout and stopping it in its tracks.

It looked away from her and Mia just caught a glimpse of Grub.

Not wanting to waste his timely distraction, she grabbed her sword, gathered herself, and lunged, running the demon through its human chest.

She ripped the blade free and hacked its head off for good measure.

Joran ran over and grabbed her shoulders. "Are you okay?"

"Bruised, but otherwise undamaged. Good timing with the adhesive vial."

"Thanks. I'm down to my last one unless we find some reagents."

They both turned and Mia grimaced. The demons had already begun to dissolve and the stink they gave off rivaled anything she'd smelled during her youth in the slums.

"Let's do what you have to with the meat and get out of here."

"You don't have to ask me twice." Joran led the way back toward Stoneheart and the others. He paused beside Grub. "Good work with the lightning. Thanks."

Grub nodded and looked away. He seemed uncomfortable with the compliment. Mia squeezed his shoulder in passing, but didn't say anything. Without his help, she'd be dead now. Joran seemed to trust him and she trusted Joran, but now that Grub had risked his life to save hers, Mia felt confident that he really was on their side. It seemed like even Stoneheart would have to acknowledge that.

An hour of work saw them on their way again. A brief stop at the bunkhouse yielded some iron vegetables of uncertain species. She figured they'd have a better idea what they'd found when she purified them. She offered to do it right away, but Joran said they should wait as anything they transformed would start to decay at once.

With their food situation at least a little bit under control and no more demons hunting for them, Bahesti led them away from the farm and deeper into the ruined empire.

Mia had no idea what they might find, but she felt confident that her sword would kill whatever got in their way.

CHAPTER 14

Samaritan found living on a diet of nothing save vinegary wine left a lot to be desired. He'd been trudging along behind Overmage and his minions for four days, maybe five. He'd lost track between the headache and empty stomach. He was actually starting to envy the metal men their lack of dietary needs, nightly sleep, and rest. Of course, an eternity in this miserable place was a pretty steep price to pay for them.

As if reading his mind, Overmage looked back. "We will reach the first village by midday. With any luck we will find you some food."

Those might have been the sweetest words Samaritan had heard since his soulmate was killed. "Did the others encounter any resistance?"

"I don't know. I command them, but our minds aren't linked. That would require access to the ether, which my curse denies."

Samaritan nodded. He hadn't made up his mind how much of what Overmage said he should believe. The man claimed to be one of the former rulers of the empire, yet what he knew and didn't know suggested someone of far lower rank. Samaritan had dealt with enough nobles to recognize someone pretending to a higher station than he deserved.

Of course, getting his brain turned to metal might well have something to do with his memory problems.

A long pull of wine slaked his thirst before promptly turning to acid in his stomach. If this went on for too much longer, he was apt to end up with an ulcer. Maybe he could steal a cure all. He'd never tried one of the miraculous potions, but felt like he deserved one after the last few weeks.

The sun—or at least he assumed the slightly brighter patch in the endless clouds was the sun—slowly climbed toward its zenith. Samaritan's mouth watered at the prospect of finding something, anything, to eat.

They topped a low rise and at the bottom, in a sheltered valley, sat a little town. All the buildings had been turned to black iron. The few people outside looked like metal statues. All in all, the place looked more like a park than somewhere people used to actually live.

An iron figure came flying out from behind one of the buildings, bounced a few times, and quickly climbed to its feet. Samaritan felt pretty certain it was one of Overmage's followers. Of course, from a distance, all the iron people looked the same to him.

"What's going on?" Samaritan asked.

The answer came a moment later when a four-foot-tall, red-skinned dwarf with short, sharp horns stalked out from behind the same building. The dwarf had massive muscles rippling under his skin. The second metal man lay limp on the ground, his ankle in the dwarf's hand as he was dragged along behind him.

"Uh-oh," Overmage said in perhaps the greatest understatement in decades. "A crimson dwarf. We summoned and bound them to serve as smiths. In hell they forge true black iron weapons. The hope was that if we used the same techniques, our own weapons would be of equal quality. This one must have broken out of his bindings."

"I deduced that myself. How do we stop him?"

"Given our combined weapons and abilities, I doubt we can." As Overmage spoke, the dwarf swung the figure in his grasp like a war hammer, slamming him into the now-recovered first minion.

Both metal men went flying. Lucky for them, they took the blows like champs, quickly getting back to their feet and charging only to be sent flying again by powerful punches.

"This could go on forever," Samaritan said. "They're too evenly matched."

"I'm open to suggestions."

"Let's go down and try talking to the demon. Perhaps we can come to a mutually beneficial agreement."

"You go right ahead," Overmage said. "I'll wait here."

That, at least, sounded like something a ruler looking to protect his own skin would say. For his part, Samaritan was so miserable he didn't really care what happened to him so long as he got a chance to look for something to eat.

Leaving Overmage quaking on the hill, he marched down to the village with the confident stride he always used to use when on a mission. Samaritan knew little about demons and none of it came firsthand. He'd read the standard church texts about how they were evil enemies of The One God and should be slain whenever encountered.

Pity the books offered no information on how to go about that.

At fifteen yards away, the dwarf demon hurled Overmage's lackeys away once more and turned his angry, crimson gaze on Samaritan. Up close, Samaritan noticed that the dwarf's beard was made of what looked like porcupine quills. An interesting if utterly useless observation.

"You look like you'll break a mite easier than the other two," the dwarf said.

At five paces away Samaritan stopped and bowed, doing his best not to let his disgust at the stink of rot surrounding the demon show. "I have no doubt you're correct about that. My name is Samaritan and I hoped we might talk."

The demon narrowed his eyes. "Talk about what?"

"Why you're here. Why we're here. How we can end this confrontation without further violence."

"You don't know much about demons, do you, human?"

"Only what I've read, but frankly, given the source of the information, I assume it was all lies. Why don't you tell me what you want? Surely tossing around those iron fools is getting boring."

"It is at that. Everything in the miserable place is boring. I've been wandering around this shithole for centuries, ever since my binding broke. I hoped it might send me back to Abaddon's hell and my rightful place at the forges. But no. Instead I'm stuck here with nothing to do but smack around metal men that don't even scream."

"That sounds frustrating. Is there no way for you to get back home?"

"Sure, I need to get killed or find a functioning hellgate. Of course, if I get killed, I'll be stuck relying on Abaddon's goodwill to restore me to my current form and position. And if you know anything about demon lords, you know they have little in the way of goodwill."

Samaritan, in fact, knew nothing about demon lords. The name Abaddon was totally new to him. Still, it came as no surprise that the ruler of Hell might not be the kindest of masters.

"Then you're looking for a hellgate?"

"Yes, sort of. The truth is, I've been from one side of the empire to the other. If there was a gate to be found, I'd have done so by now. I figure there must be one in the capital, but it's at the bottom of the bloody ocean."

Samaritan cocked his head, thoroughly intrigued by the demon. He spoke, thought, and acted just like a person, albeit a short, red, evil one. Somehow Samaritan had imagined demons to be nothing more than rampaging forces of destruction, like the serpent he woke, rather than individuals with goals and personalities.

"Is that a problem for you?" he asked. "I mean, do you need to breathe like a mortal does?"

"Not exactly, but most of my best powers are fire based and underwater they'd be useless. If the corrupt ether has warped the local wildlife to a significant degree, I'm liable to end up back in Hell the hard way without my most powerful magic." The demon cracked his knuckles. "This little chat has been a nice change of pace, but I'm going to rip your arms off now."

"One more moment, please. My companions and I are searching for some information along with a bile portal back to where I came from. I don't know if you can find a hellgate in the Tiberian Empire, but at a minimum there are many humans you can kill."

The dwarf frowned, making his quills shake. "And you want to bring me there why?"

"I hate the empire. The more of them you kill, the happier it would make me. Not a bad deal, right? At the very least you'd have a new place to explore and some chance of finding a way back to Hell."

He scratched his quills. "You're an odd human and no mistake. I do think you actually believe what you're saying. Okay, I'll join you. Should I find you've led me astray, I can always rip your arms off later. At a bare minimum, having someone to talk with will make a nice break from my usual routine."

"Splendid, I'm glad to have you along. I don't suppose you found any edible food in this village? If I'm going to make it to our destination, I need something to eat in a bad way."

The demon shrugged. "I haven't the slightest idea. Food isn't something I waste my time looking for."

That didn't surprise Samaritan, but he figured it couldn't hurt to ask. He waved Overmage down and the metal man made his cautious way closer. His minions came along from another direction even more cautiously. As far as Samaritan could tell, they appeared no worse for their fight with the demon.

When Overmage reached them, Samaritan said, "My new friend is going to be joining us. Oh, do you have a name?"

"You can call me Gomo," the dwarf said.

Samaritan bowed. Had his former superiors in the White Knights seen him showing such respect to a demon, they likely would have cut him down on the spot. "This is my traveling companion. He goes by the name Overmage. His bodyguards..."

"Are irrelevant," Overmage said. "Which of my peers summoned you, Gomo?"

"No overmage summoned me. Some second-tier wizard following instructions written by his betters and using the power of Black Bile summoned and bound me. If an actual overmage had done the job, I'd likely still be hammering out cheap imitations of the black iron swords I used to make in Hell."

Overmage shook his head and his brow drew down as if he were confused. Samaritan hadn't seen any kind of emotion on Overmage's face before this and it gave him a moment of concern. Happily, the episode ended as quickly as it started. If his only guide lost it, relying on Gomo didn't overly appeal to Samaritan.

"I need to check these buildings for food. Shouldn't take long." He left Gomo and Overmage glaring at each other.

Hopefully he could find something to fill his aching belly. Almost as important, he hoped his disagreeable companions didn't kill each other in his absence.

CHAPTER 15

Ten days of steady marching brought Joran and his party to their destination, a massive black iron fortress that loomed over them like a small mountain. The central keep had to be at least ten stories tall and the wall surrounding it five. Both structures appeared undamaged. Four towers, three of them fully intact, marked the corners of the wall. Joran had never seen a more intimidating building. On the plus side, nothing patrolled the wall and the main gate's draw-bridge was open and the portcullis up. That would make getting inside the wall at least a simple matter.

"Wow," Mia said. "I didn't know men could build things like this."

"When you have access to nearly unlimited magic via Black Bile and a large force of slave labor, you'd be amazed what's possible," Bahesti said. "But such things come at a price, as you've seen."

She nodded, but the wonder in her face didn't lessen in the least. Joran offered a genuine smile. That Mia could find a moment of joy and wonder in the midst of this hellscape didn't surprise him, but it did please him.

"So what are we waiting for?" Grub asked.

"Not a thing," Joran said. "Bahesti?"

"We can go in easily enough, but when last I visited the area, the drawbridge was closed and the portcullis down. Someone has been here and may yet be here. Do you still wish to proceed?"

"Do we have any other options?" Joran asked.

"Not nearby. The next overmage's citadel is two islands over and perhaps two weeks' travel at your pace."

"And we have no idea what we'll find." Joran shook his head. "We may as well take a look at this one as long as we're here. If we run into trouble, we can always fall back and regroup."

No one seemed overly eager to explore the fortress after Bahesti's explanation, but no one argued with Joran's decision. Of course, he knew it might not be as simple as he made out if they ran into trouble, but they'd been here for so long already that he didn't want to spend another two weeks on a gamble that might end up worse than what they had in front of them.

Bahesti set out in the lead with Mia right behind him. Maybe they'd get lucky and find that whoever came to visit had already gone home. And maybe they'd find a portal in the basement that led to Tiber and they could just go back home. If he wanted to dream, he might as well dream big.

Their boots clunked as they marched across the drawbridge and under the portcullis. An open yard separated the wall from the keep. There were no outbuildings or even the remains of them. Joran had visited a few castles and they all had outbuildings. A smithy, a barracks, something.

When Joran mentioned it Bahesti said, "The overmages liked to have everything under one roof to better keep an eye on their minions. Our rulers were not well loved, but they were heartily feared. Any attempt at betrayal would be met with instant and brutal death. My own mistress had yet to achieve the rank of overmage, but she ruled her fiefdom with the same brutal tactics."

"Probably practice for when she reached the big show," Grub muttered.

"You are precisely correct." Bahesti seemed to hold no ill will despite Grub's nasty comment. Joran really wished the dwarf could keep his distaste under wraps. For now, they were all on the same side and should act like it.

Mia's nerves rattled in Joran's brain as they looked around the training yard. If someone knew they'd arrived, they made no move to do anything about it. He figured it was fifty-fifty whether they found an empty keep or a trap. He sent a silent prayer to any power that might be listening that it was the former.

"Is there a way in besides the front door?" Joran asked.

Bahesti shook his head. "This design is easier to defend and should the overmage in residence need to escape during a siege, teleportation magic worked far better than a back door or hidden tunnel."

Right, when you could just vanish at will, it made life a lot easier.

Bahesti led them over to the front door, a tall, black iron monstrosity with a heavy knocker dangling from a skull's mouth. Just about what Joran expected the front door of an overmage's citadel to look like.

"How do we get in if it's locked?" Stoneheart asked.

Mia held up her sword. "I brought a key."

Bahesti reached out and gave the door a light push and it swung silently in. "Extreme measures, it seems, will not be necessary."

They waited a moment, but no one came charging out to try and kill them. That was about as good a sign as Joran hoped to get.

Beyond the door waited a round entry hall with another two

doors in the back wall leading deeper into the fortress. Of course, they were both closed. So little light leaked into the room that Joran had trouble making out any details. He pulled a light vial from his kit and shook it until a blue light filled the room.

It didn't reveal much. Black tiles covered the floor and the walls had been transformed into black iron. A huge iron bar on a swivel stood straight up beside the entry door which had brackets on the inside to hold the bar and seal it shut.

Should they have to retreat, Joran had no desire to deal with the bar. "Mia, would you slice those brackets off please?"

The mithril sword made quick work of them. The sound of the brackets clattering to the floor no doubt alerted everyone in the fortress that company had arrived, but that was okay. Joran wanted anyone inside to attack sooner rather than later if they were going to. Better to retreat now than after they'd begun their research.

"The dragon's magic made the fortress extra gloomy," Joran said.

"No, it always looked like this. Other than transforming the outside from stone to black iron, the dragon changed nothing. It looks exactly the way I remember on my one previous visit."

That certainly gave Joran an insight into the mind of the overmages.

A full minute passed with no sign of anyone coming to attack. Maybe they really were going to get lucky and find the place empty.

"Which door?" Joran asked.

"To the right. The left side leads to the dungeon and torture chamber."

"We definitely don't need to visit them," Mia said.

Bahesti's face made what Joran had come to recognize as his approximation of a smile. "No, we don't. Though it would doubtless be the most well-stocked torture chamber you've ever visited. The Black Iron Empire's torturers were second to none in the world."

"Hardly something to be proud of," Grub muttered.

"Oh, I'm not proud, just stating a fact. Follow me."

Bahesti led them through the right-hand door and down a long, undecorated hall. They passed a couple of closed doors without pausing.

"What are those rooms?" Joran asked.

"I haven't the least idea," Bahesti said. "The doors were closed when I came last time and my mistress didn't make any effort to find out what lay within. They could be storage, guard rooms, or anything else the mind of an overmage might conjure up. All I know for sure is they don't lead to the library."

Even holding his breath Joran heard nothing beyond the doors. He glanced at Mia and she shook her head as well. Finally, he shrugged and motioned Bahesti on.

A couple twists and turns past more closed doors and through black, empty halls led them to a set of stairs up to the second level.

Bahesti paused at the bottom. "The library takes up the entire second level. Most of it is historical data and magical research. Luckily for us, the filing system is quite thorough. We'll check the catalogue first, then the section it indicates."

"Are the books written in the language we're speaking?" Joran had a few translation potions, but if he had to give one to everyone in the group, it would use up his supply in a hurry.

"Of course. The catalogue is written in overrunes, but the books themselves are in Imperial."

"How come we use the same language as you?' Mia asked.

Bahesti shrugged. "I assume your country was once one of our provinces. If there's another explanation, I can't think of it."

Joran had never read about Tiber being part of the Black Iron Empire, but that meant nothing. The people might well have come from a province after the dragon attacked and settled in Tiber. As long as they could read the books, the rest was just a historical footnote.

Their footsteps echoed as the group climbed to the second floor. At the landing, yet another black door waited. After a brief pause to listen, Bahesti pulled it open.

Bookshelves filled to bursting with tomes beyond counting stretched as far as Joran could see. It made the imperial archive look like a merchant's private collection. He hoped the catalog was as useful as Bahesti thought, because if they had to search the old-fashioned way, they'd run out of food long before they made a dent in the collection.

It gave Joran considerable confidence when Bahesti led them straight up the central aisle to a round cabinet filled with little drawers, each marked with a character made up of vertical and horizontal lines.

"Are those the overrunes you mentioned?" Joran asked.

"That's right. I'll need some time to find the correct section."

"We'll have lunch and stay out of your way. If you need any assistance, let me know. Oh, do you want the light? I have another."

"No need. I can see perfectly well in the dark. One of the gifts that came with this new body. Strange that I should get new abilities even as I lost the ones I most valued."

"Maybe the dragon wanted you to be able to see the emptiness surrounding you even after sunset," Grub said. "It seems like the sort of thing it might enjoy."

Bahesti shrugged. "No cruelty is too great for the beast. If you'll excuse me."

Joran led the others a short distance away and they settled on the floor. Bahesti's golem kept watch while its master worked.

Stoneheart passed out preserved meat and some of the starchy vegetables Mia had purified that morning. Two days ago they'd refilled their water supply from a nasty pool that took nearly an hour to cleanse with the mithril. It tasted funny, but no one got sick.

The combination didn't make for an especially enjoyable meal, but Joran had gotten used it. The trick, he'd decided, was to eat as quickly as possible to avoid tasting the food.

"I didn't think there were this many books in the whole world," Mia said. "I had a nightmare sort of like this after we went to the archive."

Joran smiled around a mouthful of meat. Books really weren't Mia's thing. "You don't think we should come back once matters are settled and try and read them all?"

She shot him a mock glare. "No."

Turning to Grub he asked, "How about you? As a wizard, all this knowledge must tempt you."

Grub shook his head. "I want nothing from this place. Any knowledge gained from the empire can only bring evil."

Stoneheart glanced at Grub with what Joran thought might be grudging respect.

Joran agreed with the sentiment if not the reality of Grub's statement. Knowledge, in his opinion, was neither good nor evil, it just was. How the individual used it determined whether good or ill resulted.

While he finished off his starchy vegetable, Joran took a moment to survey their food supply. They'd used about a third of the meat and a quarter of the vegetables. The citadel had to have a water source, so with any luck they could refill as needed. They should be okay for a little while longer. Hopefully long enough to find what they needed and get back home.

He smiled to himself. It did no one any good to be that optimistic, but sometimes he forgot his noble training.

They finished eating, but Bahesti still showed no sign of having found what he was looking for. Maybe Joran would have time to brew up a couple of potions. He had reagents and tools in his kit, but the process took at least an hour and he couldn't stop in the middle without ruining the batch.

A faint, distant sound had Mia scrambling to her feet. "Did you hear that?"

"Sounded like it came from the floor above us," Stoneheart said.

Joran climbed more slowly to his feet. "Let's check the landing. Maybe we can see what, if anything, is coming down the stairs."

Mia marched in the lead with a stride that said anything on the other side of the door would be in trouble. Grub pulled the mithril amulet from his pocket and got ready to cast. With no mithril and little magic, Joran and Stoneheart kept back out of the way.

As soon as she reached the door, Mia put her ear to it. No jolt of anxiety hit him, so Joran assumed she heard nothing.

She looked back and raised an eyebrow.

Joran slipped his last adhesive vial out of his kit and nodded.

Mia yanked the door open and stepped out, sword raised. "Nothing out here."

"That's not a bad thing," Joran said. "As long as whatever's upstairs doesn't bother us, I'm content to leave it in peace."

Mia came back in and closed the door. "I guess. But I hate not knowing what's up there."

"Want me to take a look?" Grub asked. "With the amulet, I think I can purify enough ether to extend my vision one floor up."

"What are the odds our unknown prowler mistakes your spell for something offensive?" Joran asked.

"Unless it can see the ether, none. And even if it can, the spell literally creates a pair of magical eyes. They might be a little unsettling, but not remotely threatening."

"Sounds safe enough," Joran said. "Go ahead."

Grub took a deep breath and closed his eyes. Curious as

Joran was to see how he did it, the corruption guaranteed him a headache if he even tried to touch the ether.

Mia stood beside him and offered the sword hilt first. "You can use it if you want to take a look."

Joran smiled and rested his hand on the hilt. Pure ether surrounded him as he shifted his vision. Grub had threads running through his eyes then back out and up through the ceiling. Joran hadn't been quick enough to see the process and likely wouldn't have understood it if he had. His ignorance on the uses of magic still far outweighed his understanding.

He blinked his vision back to normal and took his hand off the sword. "Thanks. Are you okay? You still seem really jumpy."

"The demon attack at the barn didn't help." She looked around as if seeking an explanation. "It feels like everything around here wants to kill me. Like the land itself is an enemy. I've tried, but I just can't shake the feeling."

"I wonder if it's because you're in a bubble of pure ether surrounded by endless corruption. You may be struggling to acclimate to your surroundings. On the other hand, by its very nature, the corruption is trying to slowly kill us, so your feelings aren't technically wrong."

"What do I do about it?"

"I'm not certain there's anything you can do."

"I see something," Grub said, ending their conversation.

"Just one something?" Joran asked. "That's not so bad."

"You only say that because you haven't seen it. I've never come across anything like this thing, in books or my worst nightmares. It's covered in scales as thick as breast plates, has four arms, and a tail ending in a bone club bigger than General Fiendhammer's war hammer. Its back is to me and I don't want to get too close on the off chance it can see the ether."

"What's it doing?" Joran asked.

"That's the weird thing, it's just wandering around like it's lost. The noise we hear from time to time is its tail scraping on the floor."

"What's above us?"

"The room where the creature is wandering is empty. I'd guess it's a third the size of the library."

Weird hardly began to describe it, but then again, you could say that about their entire situation. "That's good enough, Grub, thank you. As long as it stays up there and doesn't bother us, we'll return the favor." Joran glanced over at Bahesti who was still going from drawer to drawer in search of the information they needed.

No need to interrupt him. When he finished would be soon enough to see if he knew anything about their upstairs neighbor.

CHAPTER 16

Two weeks of walking brought Samaritan and his companions within sight of their destination. Or at least their next obstacle, a stone bridge about a foot wide that arched over the gap between the island where he stood and the one Overmage claimed held a library with the information he needed. The bridge had no braces or reinforcements. Samaritan wasn't much of an engineer, but even he knew that it shouldn't be standing, much less be strong enough to hold anyone up. Magic had to be involved, but his limited training gave no hint as to how.

"You were right," Samaritan said. "Hopscotching across might have been better than this. How is it even still standing?"

"Some magic of the dragon's I'm sure," Overmage said.

"Wrong," Gomo said. "There's earth magic at work down there. Not sure what sort, too much corruption interfering."

"Who cares?" Overmage asked. "As long as the bridge holds us, nothing else matters."

"Don't be stupid," Gomo said. "If there's earth magic at work, and it happened after the dragon left, then something other than an imperial wizard cast the spell. If whatever did is still down there, we might be walking into a trap."

Overmage shook his head. "I didn't think demons were such cowards. With our combined power, anything that tries to harm us will quickly wish it hadn't."

They broke into a full-fledged argument, so Samaritan decided to take a lunch break. He thanked again whatever powers were watching over him for the chest of preserved food he'd found in the village where they met Gomo. A quick peek into the ether revealed what he assumed to be a preservation spell that by some miracle still functioned. He suspected the cache had been collected in case an emergency hit. He even found some water he mixed with wine to hopefully kill anything harmful living in it.

He chewed a heavily smoked but still tasty sausage while his companions went back and forth about the potential danger. At least the minions didn't feel the need to get involved. He hadn't heard them speak since the day he arrived and the pair carried him to their master. At the time he'd thought they had some personality, but now he was less certain.

They were still going at it when he finished his snack.

"Gentlemen." When they both looked at him he went on. "Unless there's another way across, I suggest we walk down there and see what's what. Bickering is getting us nowhere."

"A surprisingly sensible suggestion from a human," Gomo said. "Clearly not having a brain made of iron makes your thinking clearer."

Overmage opened his mouth like he wanted to argue some more then clanked it shut. After a second to gather himself, he said, "I'll send one of my bodyguards down. If nothing happens, we can go ourselves."

He shot the demon a look and when Gomo offered no objections pointed at the bridge. Samaritan assumed some mental command went along with it since one of the iron men stomped off in the direction indicated.

They all watched as it got closer and closer. Samaritan found he was holding his breath and forced himself to take a deep lungful of air and slowly let it out.

At last the metal man reached the base of the bridge. It turned and looked back at them as if waiting for instructions. Samaritan didn't know what he'd expected to happen, but nothing certainly wasn't it.

"You see," Overmage said. "Perfectly safe."

Gomo grunted but seemed not to have any more arguments.

The three of them, along with the second golem, set out to join the first. Three-quarters of the way to the bridge, a tremor ran through the ground.

Samaritan didn't even have a chance to shout a warning before stone bars shot up all around them, forming a perfect cage.

Gomo slammed his fist into a bar, shattering it to dust.

It reformed an instant later.

"Well, well, well. What have I caught?" The source of the voice rose out of the earth in the form of a man made of dirt and stone. He looked them over like a child might a bug caught in a jar.

Overmage stepped to the fore. "I used to rule this land. Let us go at once or face the consequences."

"What consequences?" the earthen man asked. "You're just a talking statue now. No magic, no army, no servants, no nothing. You couldn't hurt me if you wanted to."

Overmage glared and out of the corner of his eye Samaritan spotted the still-free golem running right at the earth man's back like a battering ram.

And he hit like one too.

Their captor exploded like the cell bar Gomo had struck.

Dust and dirt went everywhere.

"I warned you there would be consequences," Overmage said.

The debris reversed course and as they watched in wordless horror the earth man reformed seeming none the worse for getting blown apart.

"And I warned you that you couldn't hurt me if you wanted to." The strange entity pointed at the golem that had attacked him.

A pillar of dirt shot up under its feet and sent it flying up and over the cliff that marked the edge of the island. A loud splash sounded a moment later.

"You will suffer for that," Overmage said.

"Your pathetic threats don't impress me."

"What, exactly, do you want?" Samaritan asked.

"Finally, someone reasonable. I'm bound to this island by the wizards' magic. The artifact that serves as my anchor is on the other side of the bridge. I want you to destroy it and set me free." The earth man raised a finger before Samaritan could speak. "Lest you think of agreeing then not following through when you reach the other side, you should know that I can also manifest over there and your deaths will not be pleasant should you betray me."

"If you're so bloody powerful," Gomo said. "Why not just destroy it yourself?"

"I would, but the magic protecting the artifact has a ward that keeps summoned beings from approaching, including demons. It will fall to the human and the former overmage to complete the task."

"I don't run errands," Overmage said.

Samaritan would have backhanded the arrogant fool if he thought it would accomplish anything beyond breaking his fingers. "I will see it done. What does the artifact look like and how do I destroy it?"

"Beyond the bridge about two miles you will find a castle

with a tall, central tower. On the top floor of the tower rests a crystal the size of a melon. Breaking it should be a simple matter for anyone capable of reaching it. I recommend dropping it on the stone floor."

"That's it?" Samaritan asked. It sounded too easy.

"There are wards and, I assume, guardians. But yes, the actual task is that simple. Once the crystal is gone, I will be free to return to the elemental plane of earth and you can get on with whatever business brings you this way. Do we have a deal?"

"If we say no, I assume that painful death you mentioned will be our punishment," Samaritan said.

"Correct. Though I doubt I can kill the metal men, I can bury them so deep it will take a century for them to dig themselves free."

Samaritan nodded. "Then I accept your terms."

The earth man turned to Overmage. "And you?"

"Very well. I have too much to do to waste any more time on this."

The walls of their cage vanished back into the earth. "Then I bid you safe journey, at least until you free me. After that, I couldn't care less what happens to you."

The figure melted back into the ground as smooth and silent as it rose. Samaritan assumed its presence lingered to watch them, but assuming they didn't break their word, he figured they should be safe enough.

At least he hoped so.

———

Crossing the bridge ended up being easier than Samaritan had feared when he first saw it. Despite the narrowness, his every footfall had seemed sure and steady. He had no proof, but assumed that the earth spirit—that's what Gomo said the thing was—steadied them to ensure they made it to the citadel in one piece.

That had been an hour ago. Now they were following a ripple in the dirt across an open field. In the distance, a black castle with a tower jutting out of the center thrust into the sky. A fairly high wall as black as everything else around here surrounded the main keep. Samaritan had seen his share of fortifications in the empire, but nothing close to as intimidating as this one.

"Is it safe to assume that this is the same citadel where we'll find the library you mentioned?"

Overmage nodded. "It doesn't surprise me that one of my peers summoned that spirit. He probably used it to increase crop yields in his territory."

"How civic minded."

Overmage continued as if Samaritan hadn't spoken. "If one of the other territories had a bad harvest, he'd be able to trade excess food for votes during council meetings. It was a less violent way to increase one's power than most of us preferred, but no less effective for all that."

That sounded more like what he expected.

They marched on in silence until at last they stood in front of a closed drawbridge. A moat filled with sharped iron stakes surrounded the citadel. Getting in, it seemed, would not be as easy as he'd hoped.

"What now?" Gomo asked.

"Can't you teleport in?" Overmage asked.

"You know as well as I do that all these fortresses are protected by teleportation wards. Maybe try not saying something so stupid next time."

Overmage looked like he wanted to argue, but mercifully cut the words off.

"I believe I can be of assistance," the earth spirit said.

The ground humped up under the second golem and before

anyone could say anything a pillar of dirt shot up, sending the golem flying up and over the wall like a catapult stone. Hopefully it was every bit as durable as Samaritan believed.

Overmage focused on the castle and said, "Lower the drawbridge!"

Nothing happened for a minute, then two. Finally a loud clanking filled the air and the drawbridge slowly lowered across the moat of spikes. At the end of it a portcullis of black iron blocked entry.

"Raise the portcullis!" Overmage said.

"Not the brightest things in the world, are they?" Gomo asked.

"Perhaps not," Overmage said. "But they've been of greater use than you so far."

Gomo's quills shook as he chuckled. "Don't worry, if it comes to a fight, you'll be glad to have me along."

At last, before another full-fledged argument had a chance to break out, the portcullis rose up out of sight.

"Thank the universe." Samaritan led the way across the bridge, as much to put some distance between himself and his companions as out of any desire to be the first one inside.

Not that there was much to see inside. The courtyard was nothing but black dirt. No outbuildings, no real training area, just a twenty-yard patch of nothing separating the wall from the fortress. And what a fortress. The central tower had to be ten stories tall and forty yards on a side. A pair of heavy iron doors blocked access to the interior.

Samaritan turned to Overmage. "Are all the citadels like this one?"

"No. Each of us had our own preferences and each citadel reflects that. My own, for instance..." He trailed off as if unable to remember what his tower had looked like. "Doesn't matter. It's gone now. Come along, we have work to do."

Samaritan shrugged, not overly interested in what his

companion's citadel had looked like. He glanced at Gomo and the demon spun his finger in a circle beside his head and rolled his eyes to indicate what he thought about Overmage. The demon might well be right. Something was definitely off about Overmage.

"Do you feel any discomfort?" Samaritan asked. "Summoned beings are supposed to be barred from this area."

Gomo shook his head. "I can sense the wards, but they're localized near the top of the tower. I'll be fine until we get closer. Why do you care?"

"I don't especially, but if there's danger above, I'd just as soon have as many fighters as possible ready to meet it. My sword is nothing but plain steel and my magic is weak and nearly unusable with all the corruption. I fear if it came down to me defeating anything stronger than an ordinary human, I'd be in trouble. And since I arrived, I've seen nothing resembling a normal human."

Gomo chuckled again. "As humans go, you seem reasonable. Give me your sword."

Taken aback by the suggestion, Samaritan hesitated. But only for a second. His sword was useless. Even if Gomo destroyed it, he wouldn't be that much worse off.

He drew the sword and handed it over to the demon.

"This is fine work for humans. There's some minor magic making the metal stronger and sharper than ordinary steel. Not much of an advantage and certainly no match for even the phony black iron swords I made here, but still impressive for mortals. That said, there is definitely room for improvements."

"What's the delay?" Overmage shouted from beside the open fortress door.

Samaritan hadn't even noticed how he got it open. Maybe he knew some trick his fellows used to secure them. Or maybe it was just unlocked. Either way, Gomo ignored the shout. The demon's eyes were glowing like coals in a forge. A moment later Samaritan's sword started glowing the same color.

The metal seemed to soak up whatever magic Gomo used. The process continued for nearly a minute. Samaritan peeked through the ether a few times, but had no real idea what Gomo was doing.

At last, the glow from Gomo's eyes vanished followed by the one surrounding the sword. Gomo handed it back. "There. Now you should be able to at least cut any save the most powerful enemies. The magic will only last twelve hours, then I'll need to renew it."

The weapon felt no different in Samaritan's hand. "What did you do?"

"I infused it with the power of hellfire. Just a tiny bit. Anything more would have melted your sword to slag. If there's a fight and you're standing at my back, I'd just as soon have you able to hurt whatever guardians we might face."

That certainly made more sense than the demon helping out of the goodness of his heart. Assuming he even had a heart, much less any goodness.

"Whatever your reasons, I thank you for your consideration. I think Overmage is getting impatient."

"Like I care what the stuck-up statue wants."

Still, Gomo made no objection when Samaritan led the way over to the fortress entrance.

"Finally." Overmage waved them inside where the golem waited and slammed the door. "Let's get to the library and start researching."

Samaritan raised an eyebrow. "Don't you think we should make sure the fortress is secure then complete the earth spirit's task? Once that's done, we'll have all the time in the world to find the answers we need, plus we won't have to worry about something nasty sneaking up on us."

"I am in charge of this expedition," Overmage said. "You do what I say, not the other way around."

Samaritan waited, impassive, as Overmage tried to glare him into submission. He might better have stared at the wall for all the good it did.

"Fine. We search the citadel, smash the spirit's crystal, then return to the library. I'm only doing this to help you focus on the research, nothing more."

Samaritan forced himself not to smile and instead offered a mocking bow. "I appreciate your consideration. Thank you."

Overmage grumbled something unintelligible then touched a spot on the wall. The corridor ahead of them lit up under the glow of crystals embedded in the ceiling. That was a handy trick. Certainly more useful than hanging alchemical lights from the ceiling.

As they left the little entry area behind and moved deeper into the fortress Samaritan asked, "Any idea what sort of defenses we're apt to run into?"

"Every overmage had their preferences and I can't even remember which of my fellows lived here. But don't worry, there won't be anything too dangerous in the public areas of the citadel. Once we reach the third floor, that's when the problems begin. It mostly depends on whether the over-mage that lived here was home when the dragon attacked or out."

Before Samaritan had a chance to ask his next question, they stopped in front of a closed black iron door on the right-hand wall.

Overmage said, "If you're so determined to search the entire citadel before we get to work, we may as well start here. The door shouldn't be locked."

Samaritan drew his now-enchanted sword and pulled the door open.

A hint of motion provided his only warning.

He got his sword up and between him and whatever leapt at his throat.

The weight of it still bore him to the floor.

All he saw was a muzzle filled with fangs dripping slobber snapping at his face while he fought with all his might to keep it from biting his nose off.

The weight vanished when Gomo kicked the beast off of him, sending it flying down the hall.

Samaritan scrambled to his feet, breathing hard. Ten paces away, the beast—it looked like a six-legged wolf with no tail and burning red eyes—righted itself and got ready to charge again.

Gomo stepped forward and pointed at the monster.

It exploded in a shower of gore, staining the walls with greenish-black ichor.

Samaritan rounded on Overmage. "I thought you said there were no guardians or wards on the first two floors."

"There aren't, but I didn't say a wandering hellhound that broke free of its binding might not be in the area. How am I supposed to know what sort of pets my fellow overmage kept?"

He wanted to shout in the arrogant bastard's face, but knew it would do no good. Instead, he slammed his sword back into its sheath. "Let's keep moving."

Finally, a bit of good luck found them and they managed to finish clearing the ground floor and the second-floor library without encountering any more demons. It looked like it took everything Overmage had to pull himself out of the library and back to the landing to begin the climb up to the third floor. Having seen the number of books stuffing the shelves, Samaritan wouldn't have been surprised to find that locating the information they needed was the bigger task.

No wards glowed on the first step, but Overmage still hesitated. At last, he turned to Samaritan and Gomo. "This is where the real danger begins. Prepare yourselves. The home of an overmage holds dangers beyond counting."

CHAPTER 17

It never occurred to Joran that the most dangerous thing he would face in an overmage's citadel would be boredom. But after hours of sitting with nothing to do beyond watching Bahesti go from drawer to drawer searching for the section of the library that held the secret of the dragon's resting place, he was about ready to pull his hair out.

At least the creature upstairs hadn't shown any inclination to come down and trouble them. Aside from the occasional thump of its tail you couldn't have asked for a more agreeable neighbor.

"We should've brought cards," Mia said.

Joran smiled and certainly couldn't argue. Not that they'd exactly had a ton of time to plan before their journey.

"What do you think is taking him so long anyway?" Grub asked.

"Given the sheer volume of texts, we have to expect that it's going to take some time to read through it all. I'm not thrilled about it, but it's not like we have a lot of other options. I'm sure Bahesti is working as fast as he can. At least we're reasonably safe at the moment."

"Sure, safe. As long as that thing upstairs doesn't get as bored as we are and decide to come down here for a snack," Grub said.

"I'd welcome a fight if I thought my axe had any hope of hurting that thing," Stoneheart said.

"We've made it this far without losing anyone," Joran said. "I'd just as soon not break our streak if we can avoid it."

"I have it!" Bahesti shouted from the library catalog.

Thank The One God. Joran stood and straightened, his back popping. "What did you find?"

"A journal written by one of the overmage's assistants. It is supposed to chronicle the entire effort to find the source of the Black Bile. I had assumed that no one survived the journey, but I'm delighted to find I was wrong."

"Wait," Joran said. "I thought the dragon destroyed the empire immediately after being woken up. How did this assistant make it back here to file his journal?"

"I haven't the slightest idea," Bahesti said. "I wasn't personally involved in the mission to find the source of the Black Bile. Assuming the assistant was a mage of some ability, he might've teleported back here immediately. I suppose it is also possible that the dragon needed some time to wake up before unleashing its wrath on the empire."

"Sounds like a lot of hogwash to me," Grub said.

"Whether it is or it isn't," Bahesti said. "I've found nothing else that gives even a hint of where to find the dragon. If you don't wish to take a look at it, we may as well leave now and head for the nearest bile portal."

Joran shot Grub a dark look. The dwarf's negativity was getting on his nerves.

"Of course we're going to take a look. We didn't come all this way for nothing. By the way, we've discovered something upstairs." Joran described the monster Grub saw. "Does that sound like anything you're familiar with?"

Bahesti shook his head. "No, but the horrors created by the

overmages are beyond counting. The thing upstairs could be anything from a summoned demon to some creation powered by the Black Bile. Leaving it alone as long as it leaves us alone is the correct decision. Follow me, we'll see if we can find the journal."

They walked past bookcase after bookcase. Bahesti's gaze darted left and right. Joran tried to figure out what he was looking at, and finally decided it was the little markings burned into the edge of the bookshelves. Joran had no idea what they meant, but as long as their guide did nothing else mattered.

At last, Bahesti stopped in front of one of the bookcases. "This is it. The journal should be marked with a golden O with a J in the center."

"Got it." Mia took a book down from the second shelf from the top and handed it to Joran.

He opened it and scanned the first page. Just as Bahesti promised, the book was written in Imperial. He read the first three pages before looking up at Bahesti. "You don't mind if I read this first, do you?"

"Not in the least. I have no desire to know more about the dragon than I already do. In fact, if I could forget what I already know, it wouldn't upset me in the least."

Joran nodded and turned his attention back to the book. For a man who thought he would soon be dead, Bahesti's attitude made sense.

He'd barely made it through a rather tedious description of the preparations the overmages made for their journey when Mia grabbed his shoulder. "I heard something."

"The creature upstairs?" he asked.

She shook her head. "No, this came from below."

"The dungeon?" Joran asked.

"Possibly," Bahesti said. "While the dungeon and the torture chamber take up the bulk of the space in the basement in most citadels, there are also likely laboratories and a bile pit. I've never been to the basement personally, so there could be just about anything."

There were more noises, this time definitely from upstairs.

"The door!" Mia sprinted toward the library entrance.

Joran tucked the book into his kit. "I'm taking this."

"There's no one among the living who will care," Bahesti said.

Joran was more concerned about some sort of magical curse. He set the thought aside and hurried to catch up with Mia. He found her standing beside the closed door, her ear pressed to it.

"Anything?"

"It's on the steps coming down," Mia whispered. "I can still hear the other thing downstairs, but it's more distant."

There was a collective gasp as they held their breath to listen. Clunk, clunk, clunk went the monster's steps down from the third floor. It sounded insanely heavy. If, The One God forbid, it went through the steps, how were Joran and his companions going to make it to the exit?

He did his best not to think about it. Whatever happened, it was out of his control. As long as they didn't get into a fight, nothing else mattered at the moment.

The heaviest thud yet sounded on the landing beyond the door. Mia looked at him with wide eyes and mouthed the words, "It's right outside."

He nodded and touched his finger to his lips. Was it possible the creature didn't even know they were there? He sincerely hoped so. After what seemed like a long time, the monster started moving again, headed for the first floor.

As one they let out a sigh of relief. That had been far too close.

"If there are two monsters downstairs, how are we going to get out of here?" Stoneheart asked.

"Maybe we'll get lucky and they'll kill each other. Then we can just step over their bodies on the way out," Grub said.

Joran forced himself not to smile. With the way their luck had been going, there was no way they were going to catch such a huge break.

"Best-case scenario," Mia said. "One of the monsters kills the other but gets wounded badly enough that I can finish it off. Anything else is liable to leave us with a hard fight."

A near-deafening crash was followed by tremendous roars. At least the monsters weren't friends plotting the best way to come up here and kill them all.

"I need to see what I'm dealing with." Mia reached for the door handle.

Joran caught her wrist. "Are you crazy? That thing could squish you by accident."

"If I can see how they fight, it will give me a huge advantage if I have to go up against one, or, The One God forbid, both of them. Don't worry, I'm not going to get that close."

As far as Joran was concerned, even being on the same floor with an iron-scaled monster was too close. However, he trusted that Mia knew what she was doing.

He let go of her wrist and nodded. "Good luck."

She smiled, opened the door, and slipped out of sight.

———

Mia snuck down the stairs, quiet as a mouse. She didn't know why she went to all the trouble to not make a sound. The crashes of the battling monsters would drown out the creak or crunch of a bad step. In fact, the roars and heavy blows were starting to hurt her ears and she still hadn't even gotten to the first-floor landing.

A particularly heavy crash nearly sent her falling down the final five steps. It felt like the monsters were going to tear the tower down around their ears. Three quick strides brought her to the landing. A wavering red light allowed her to see enough to keep moving. Where had it come from? When they'd got here, it had been pitch black beyond the doorway.

She shook her head. It didn't matter. The fact that she could see was enough.

Feeling tremendously better with solid floor under her feet, Mia snuck down the hall toward the entry area. It sounded like that was where the monsters were battling. She hadn't seen another chamber big enough to accommodate something the size that Grub described.

At the end of the hall, she froze and stared, barely able to comprehend what she saw before her. One monster, which had the scales and tail, battled another one that looked like someone had stuck the severed head of a bull on the body of a human giant maybe eight feet tall made of black iron. Joran might know what to call them, but she could barely comprehend their existence. It seemed to her that things like this had no place in the natural world. Assuming you could call this ruined land part of the natural world.

The creature with the bull's head landed a right cross to the other one powerful enough to shatter a watch tower. The second monster barely staggered before turning and sending the bull-headed one flying with a blow from its massive tail.

They went back and forth a few times, neither seeming to be able to gain an advantage. Their black iron skins protected them from taking any damage. Mia ran a finger along the hilt of her sword. That iron wouldn't protect them from her. Getting in close enough to land a fatal blow would be the real challenge.

After several minutes of pointless clashes, the one with the tail leapt and drove the bull-headed statue to the floor. It proceeded to smash its forehead into the bull's head continuously until its opponent's skull had been flattened like a pancake and it no longer moved.

The scaled monster straightened and turned to look in her direction. Its forehead had taken some damage but for the most part it appeared perfectly intact and ready for another battle. Its head shifted and glowing white eyes focused right on her.

Mia swallowed hard. It knew she was here. Maybe it had known all along.

No sense trying to hide now. She drew her sword and stepped out into the open. If she had to fight the thing, she might as well get it over with.

They stared at each other, neither wanting to make the first move.

At last, she took a step toward it and the monster backed up a step keeping the distance between them equal.

Mia frowned. She'd been expecting it to charge. A single swing of its tail would be enough to reduce her to a red pulp. Instead it seemed hesitant to engage. Did the creature recognize her sword as a threat? She didn't know and wasn't entirely sure what to do about it.

"Can you understand me?" she asked.

It knelt, and slowly reached out into the space between them. Carefully, slowly, it carved shapes into the stone tile. Mia didn't recognize them. Some sort of writing for sure but not one she had seen before. It looked different than the markings from the library upstairs. Maybe Joran would recognize them.

"I don't know what you're trying to say. I'm going to go upstairs and get my friends. Okay?"

The monster stood up slowly and backed away so that it was nearly touching the opposite wall. It seemed to be going out of its way not to do anything threatening. That had to be the strangest part of the whole encounter. When it attacked the other thing with such violence, she'd been certain that as soon as it finished off its first opponent, it would turn on her. Mia didn't understand what was happening, but she was glad not to have to fight it.

She sheathed her sword and waited a moment. Still it made no move to attack. With a final confused look, Mia turned away from the monster and hurried back to the steps. She barely made it halfway up when she met Joran coming down.

"Are you okay? What's going on?" he asked.

"I'm fine. As for what's going on, I'm not entirely sure. The one from upstairs crushed the one from downstairs. As soon as it was finished it looked right at me, drew something on the floor, and made no move to attack."

"That's... unexpected. What did it draw?"

"A word I believe, but I didn't recognize any of the letters. I thought you might take a look."

"I'd be happy to. But I think we should fetch the others first. If it changes its mind, I don't want to have to go back for them."

Five minutes later, the entire group stood in the entry hall. The scaled monster remained beside the back wall where she'd left it. It looked at them with its odd, glowing eyes but didn't move.

"Why are we fooling around with this thing?" Grub asked. "Let's just get out of here while the getting is good."

"It could've attacked me, but it didn't. I don't know why, but it seems like it might be worth the time to try and figure it out." Mia couldn't say why she felt almost an obligation to the monster. Somehow she felt drawn to it, like she should help it if she could.

"A few minutes one way or the other isn't going to make or break us," Joran said.

He stepped out into the entry room, keeping a wary eye on the monster that remained as still as the statue it resembled. Joran walked around the markings, studying them from all angles. At last he looked up at Mia.

"I recognize them. They taught us at least the basics of this language in college. The church called it the language of angels. It says 'help.'"

Joran could hardly believe it when Mia returned and told him what had happened with the monsters downstairs. When he saw the writing in a language he associated with angels, he'd been even more confused. The truth was he considered angels as much of a fiction as he did The One God himself. That was no doubt foolish given that he knew beyond a doubt that demons were real. His bitterness toward the church and their lies had affected his thinking in a negative way. He couldn't let that happen again lest he make a fatal mistake.

While he understood his own bias in this matter, what he couldn't understand was Mia's strong feelings toward the creature. Through their link he understood that she wanted to help it. What he couldn't figure out was why. He wondered if she understood herself. Not that it mattered; if something was important to his soulmate, then it was important to him.

Unfortunately, important or not, he had no idea how to help the creature. He looked across the entryway at it and frowned. Maybe it knew how they could help.

Joran closed half the distance between them and looked up at the scaled creature. "How can we help you?"

Moving with exaggerated slowness, it hooked a finger under one of the scales covering its body and tugged. Nothing happened. After a moment it did it again to equally little effect.

"You want us to remove the scales?"

It nodded and pointed at Mia. Or more specifically at her sword.

"Yes, Mia's sword can cut through the black iron. Is that what you need her to do?"

It nodded again.

He waved Mia over and explained what the creature wanted. "Are you up to giving it a try?"

"You don't think I'll hurt it, do you?"

"At this point I don't know what to think. All I know for sure is that it wants you to remove the scales. If you don't want to, I'm not sure what else we can do for it."

"Since it asked for our help, I guess it would be kind of dumb not to at least try and do what it wants." Mia drew her sword and turned to the monster. "Where do you want me to start?"

Three long strides and the creature stood directly in front of them. This close, Joran could finally appreciate just how big it was. His head barely came to its waist and he guessed it weighed at least ten tons.

It took a knee and the floor shook with the impact. With the same exaggerated slowness it used earlier, the creature touched a scale on its side just about shoulder height to Mia. No ambiguity there.

She took a step and lined up with the scale it wanted cut. Even from a few steps away, Joran heard her take a deep breath. The mithril sword snapped out and sliced the scale cleanly off the monster's body. As it fell to the floor, a white light shot out, nearly blinding him.

Joran threw an arm out to cover his eyes.

Crashes mingled with the screech of iron. Joran scrambled back, instinctively trying to avoid getting crushed.

When silence fell again, he slowly lowered his arm. Uncertain he was actually seeing what he saw, Joran rubbed his eyes and looked again. A being made of pure light floated in the center of the entryway surrounded by the remains of the iron shell that had imprisoned it. The angel, for it could be nothing else, looked like a naked man with the wings of a dove. It may well have been the most perfect being Joran had ever seen.

Mia stared at it, seemingly enraptured.

Thank you, mortals. A voice that exuded warmth, kindness, and love appeared in Joran's mind. He had no doubt that the voice originated from the angel in front of him.

He moved to stand beside Mia and put a hand on her shoulder. That seemed to snap her out of whatever trance she'd been in. She looked at him with awe plain on her face. He couldn't deny feeling something similar himself.

I feared I would never be free of that cursed metal. Heaven must be looking out for me. How else to explain someone with the only weapon capable of freeing me showing up in my prison?

"Glad I could help," Mia said.

"How did you end up in such a wretched situation?" Joran asked.

A human wizard with more arrogance and power than wisdom summoned me here. As far as I could tell, his only purpose was to find out if he could trap me in a shell of black iron. As soon as he succeeded, he bound me to pace forever on the third floor and I never saw him again. Once the spell broke, I had no way to free myself of the shell, so I simply kept pacing until I sensed your arrival.

"If you knew we were here," Joran said. "Why not make contact directly?"

Amusement washed over Joran. *Had I attempted to speak with you, looking as I did, would you have given me a chance or simply run for your life?*

Joran and Mia shared a look.

"Fair point," Joran said. "Your captor certainly didn't give you a particularly divine appearance."

No. The overmages, for all their power and skill with magic, were little more than insane, demon-worshipping monsters. This world's dragon did its people a favor by killing them all.

Joran's heart raced. This was his chance to learn about the dragon from somebody that was around when it appeared. He might never get a better chance. "Can you tell me about the dragon? Another madman has appeared and hopes to use it to wipe out my home country. Any clue you can give me that would help me stop him would be welcome."

I don't know where it lives. I can tell you that its power is beyond anything you can imagine. In your mind I saw the name The One God. Though it is not real, it may be based on an entity that is or was. The Creator forged the universe and then died defending it from his brother The Destroyer. The race of angels was born from The Creator's blood. The race of demons rose from the blood of The Destroyer. And the race of true dragons was born from the mingling of their blood. Your world's true dragon is almost pure Destroyer. The only reason it doesn't obliterate the world is that it would die along with all of you. Nothing good can come from waking it.

That bit of information would give Joran plenty to think about for the rest of his life. But it didn't really help him with his current problem. "I guess my question is, should we fail to stop Samaritan from waking the dragon, is there any way to stop it from destroying my country?"

I know it isn't what you want to hear, but the truth is, there's no way, no power on your world capable of stopping the dragon should it wake.

The angel started to waver and shimmer like it was about to disappear.

Best of luck to you mortals. May the light of heaven shine upon you.

And with that the angel vanished. Joran found its absence left him feeling like something precious had been taken from him. No doubt that was just the weight of his problems settling back across his shoulders. It seemed there would be no divine intervention to save them.

"That was… something," Mia said.

"It certainly was, though I admit I wish it had been something a bit more helpful. Learning the dragon's origin but not how to stop it does us no good. We're stuck here with the same problems as before."

"What the bloody hell was that thing?" Grub asked as he and the others hurried over to join Joran and Mia.

"An angel," Joran said. He explained what the angel had told them. "Fascinating as the information was, it didn't help our situation much. We need to get home and the sooner the better. Bahesti, how far to the bile portal?"

"The one that I believe leads to the general vicinity of your homeland is northeast of here on the next island over. Ten days', perhaps two weeks' walk."

Longer than Joran would have liked, but it was what it was. "Does anyone know what time it is?"

"About two hours after noon," Stoneheart said.

Joran shot him an inquiring look.

"When you live underground, you get good at keeping track of the time without the sun's help."

Yet another thing Joran had never even given a passing thought to. "That gives us about four hours of light. I say we put as much distance between us and this place as possible."

No one objected and they set out with Bahesti once more in the lead. It seemed impossible, but Joran felt the pressure even more acutely now. Samaritan had to be stopped no matter what. Lives beyond counting depended on it.

CHAPTER 18

An overmage's citadel, at least according to the last living overmage, contained dangers beyond counting. Samaritan and his companions had climbed six levels so far and had yet to encounter so much as a magical ward. In fact, they encountered nothing of particular interest, assuming undifferentiated stretches of black iron and stone weren't your style of choice. Of course, that didn't mean they wouldn't run into some later, but so far the tower defenses didn't especially impress him.

Not that Samaritan had any intention of complaining. Only fools sought out dangers for their own sake. He preferred to avoid them as much as possible. After all, if he died, his revenge died with him.

On the seventh-floor landing Gomo stopped. "I can go no further."

Samaritan peeked into the ether and found a ceiling of dark energy blocking the way. Since he felt nothing, he assumed that the ward affected only summoned creatures, just as the earth spirit said.

"Hopefully we won't be long," Samaritan said.

Overmage shook his head. "There has to be more than this. None my fellows would leave their home so unprotected."

He sounded confused; an alarming trend Samaritan had noticed in the metal man lately. At least his confusion hadn't led them off the ultimate path. If he got confused by some minor surprise, well, Samaritan wouldn't claim to care all that much.

The two of them, along with the remaining golem, started up to the eighth floor.

"There should be lethal wards everywhere," Overmage muttered. "Guardian beasts should be opposing us at every step. What in the world has happened here?"

"Does it matter?" Samaritan asked. "As long as we complete the earth spirit's task and find the information we need, who cares about the rest?"

"It's the principle of the thing. There's a certain pride that comes with being an overmage. You don't just leave your citadel unprotected like this."

They reached the eighth landing and started up to the ninth and still no lethal dangers.

"It's been hundreds of years," Samaritan said. He didn't know why he went to the trouble of trying to reassure Overmage, but he didn't have anything better to do so why not? "Without proper maintenance, even magic breaks down eventually. Why should an overmage's citadel be any different?"

Overmage looked back over his shoulder. "We were the mightiest wizards in the empire. It should make a difference."

When he looked away Samaritan rolled his eyes. With an ego like that, Overmage would fit right in with the imperial nobility.

On the tenth floor, no wall or door separated the landing from the rest of the room. And that's all it was: a single, huge room. In the center rested the crystal on a metal stand, just as the spirit said. What the spirit hadn't mentioned, and probably knew nothing about, was the black iron statue of a giant with the head of a crocodile standing halfway between the orb and the steps. Even knowing as little as he did about the Black Iron Empire, Samaritan felt certain that thing would come to life and try to kill them should they attempt to destroy the crystal.

"At last," Overmage said. "An iron beastman statue. They were among the higher-level magical guardians popular with my fellows."

"I'm happy you're happy, but how do we get past it without getting crushed?"

"We don't. The iron beastmen aren't especially fast, but they are tough and relentless. I don't know what this one's activation parameters are, but once triggered, it won't stop until the ones that activated it are dead."

Even though he'd expected it, Overmage's explanation didn't please him. Samaritan considered his options and liked none of them. About twenty paces separated him from the crystal. He still had his dagger, but that was a long throw.

A quick glance at Overmage and his golem gave him a better idea. "Why don't you send your bodyguard to smash the crystal? It's a black iron statue the same as the beastman. It might not register as a threat."

"I have only one left. Should it be destroyed, I will be defenseless."

Samaritan wanted to slap a hand to his face. Overmage was as durable and unkillable as the golem. He needed no bodyguard in his current form. He couldn't even use magic, so that offered no excuse. No doubt the ego of a former ruler spoke more than anything practical.

"So that's a no?"

"It certainly is."

"Do you have any other suggestions?"

"You could run over to the crystal, smash it, and hope that the magic binding the guardian construct to the object it protects breaks and keeps it from activating."

"What are the odds of that working?" Samaritan asked.

"Not especially good. More likely the beastman will go berserk and try to crush everything in its path until destroyed."

"So do you have any useful suggestions?"

Overmage's shoulders creaked as he shrugged. "I warned you of the dangers and you doubted me. Now you see just how dangerous an overmage's citadel can be."

He seemed entirely too pleased with the situation given that it stood in the way of them completing their mission.

Samaritan turned away from his ever-more-useless partner and considered his options. None of them were good and all of them involved getting around the guardian of the crystal. Assuming Overmage actually knew what he was talking about, avoiding the monster once it came to life hopefully wouldn't be too huge of a problem. Having it chase them all around the citadel, on the other hand, would be a huge problem. And it looked like it would make it down the stairs despite the tight fit.

To hell with it. Standing around thinking would accomplish nothing. Gathering himself, he darted into the room.

He barely managed three steps before the beastman groaned to life.

It stomped a foot down directly in his path.

Samaritan lunged around it and then back on to his chosen path.

Only ten steps separated him from the crystal.

A black hand big enough to envelop him from knees to neck swept down.

He slid under it, sprang to his feet, and kept going.

Five more strides.

The beastman roared and Samaritan feared he might go deaf.

He didn't let the pain slow him.

Two strides from the crystal he drew his sword and swung.

The sphere shattered like glass.

He kept running toward the back wall.

The beastman stomped its feet like a child whose favorite toy just got broken. It struck the floor with such force that Samaritan staggered and nearly lost his footing.

If that happened, he was dead.

At last he made it to the far wall. Now he had to hope that Overmage actually knew as much about these things as he claimed. If he was all ego, this was going to end badly.

"Hey!" He shouted and waved his arms. "I broke your precious orb. What are you going to do about it?

The beastman's angry glowing gaze turned to focus on him. It pawed the floor like a bull, lowered its head, and charged.

The top of its head was level with Samaritan's chest.

This had seemed like a better plan when he first came up with it.

Well, he couldn't exactly back out now.

Samaritan held his breath and waited.

The monster drew closer at a terrifying rate.

At the last possible moment, he dropped to his knees. Its tooth-filled snout passed over his head close enough that it brushed his hair.

An instant later it hit the back wall with the force of a battering ram.

Iron screamed as it bent outward. The beastman roared and flailed, but found nothing to catch itself on. Samaritan turned in time to see it crash into the courtyard.

To his absolute horror, the monster started to climb to its feet. One arm had bent the wrong way and some teeth had snapped off, but other than that it appeared intact.

When it got to its feet, the ground shifted under it. Over the course of about ten seconds, it sank into the dirt until it was out of sight. A small figure rose out of the dirt, threw Samaritan a wave, and vanished in a puff of dust.

He moved away from the hole in the wall and slumped to the ground. That had been far too close.

"Clever thinking," Overmage said from behind him. "Though if the earth spirit hadn't seen fit to lend a hand, we would have been in serious trouble when we got ready to leave."

Samaritan wiped the sweat from his brow. "All's well that ends well. What do you say we collect Gomo and return to the library?"

"Splendid idea." Overmage actually sounded pleased about something for a change. "With all the distractions eliminated, we can get back to our important work. Finding the dragon's hiding place and how to wake it up."

Samaritan forced himself wearily to his feet. Yes, and most importantly, how to convince it to destroy the Tiberian Empire.

———

Samaritan had learned to do research in college and later at his ruined tower it became a necessity if he wanted to better figure out how to use his power. But despite that, he never learned how to enjoy it. Heaven only knew how many hours of reading in the library with Overmage and Gomo reinforced his dislike to the point that he almost would have preferred to fight another construct.

He tossed his most recent book, a slim folio describing a failed mission to find the source of the Black Bile, onto the table he sat beside. That was the third book he'd read to no avail. Swallowing a yawn, he reached for the next one in the pile.

"I have it!" Overmage said from the opposite side. "We hid a seeking device in the colonies—that is the continent you came from. It generates large amounts of corruption and so should be easy to locate magically. Once we reach the bile portal, it's just a matter of finding it and letting the device lead us to the dragon."

"If they had already found it, why didn't the overmages just say where? Forcing us to repeat their journey makes no sense."

Overmage touched his head as if in pain. "Perhaps the others were killed before they had the chance. I've lost so much since the transformation, but I'm sure the device described here is what we need to find."

Samaritan held out his hand. "May I see it?"

Overmage clutched the book to his chest. "Do you not trust me?"

"Trust is a tricky thing. Given what's at stake, I'd prefer to confirm the facts with my own eyes."

The metal man shrugged and held out the book. "I marked the page."

Samaritan opened then flipped a few pages back from the marker to what looked like the start of the entry. Everything looked good. The author mentioned the quest for the source of the bile and how the overmages worked together to craft the seeking orb. A page further on, he frowned. No mention about how the device made it safely back to its hiding place after the dragon wiped the overmages out. Or, for that matter, who had written the stupid journal in the first place.

He got to the marked page and read the description of the orb's location, a cave hidden by magic near the east coast. The details looked right, but the whole thing sounded off to him. On the other hand, it wasn't like he had so many options. One way or the other he needed to get back. Every day he stayed here, he felt his body getting a little weaker and he doubted the preserved food was the primary cause.

"I found the location of the bile portal," Gomo said from deeper in the library where he'd been studying a map of the bile network. A moment later the demon came stomping up to their table, a torn piece of parchment in his hand. "It's one island over."

Samaritan nodded, brushing his uncertainty aside. For better or worse, he'd made his decision. "Let's go. It's time to find a dragon."

CHAPTER 19

When Gaius joined the White Knights and went through six months of intense weapons training, he thought he knew what it meant to be tired. Three weeks of walking or riding twenty hours a day taught him that in fact he hadn't had a clue what tired meant.

He did now. Gaius passed through the gates of Tiber twenty minutes ago with no issues. Even an exhausted White Knight commanded the respect of the city guards. Though looking back on it, maybe they should have been a bit more reluctant to let someone in just because they wore a white uniform.

Dismissing the stupid, random thought, Gaius slapped himself on both cheeks and focused on the gray stone towers of the First Church of The One God. Five more minutes should see him through the doors. Whether he made it in to see the pope was another matter altogether. The ultimate success or failure of his mission came down to one simple question: would Commander Cossus's amulet get the respect he said it would?

Gaius had no idea what would happen, but he hoped whoever he spoke to gave him permission to wait for a response in one of the pews. Even a hard wooden bench would feel like a feather mattress right now.

He passed people, he felt certain, but didn't see them. An enemy could have cut his throat and Gaius doubted he would've noticed.

Death might even be a welcome rest.

His jaw clenched and he focused. He didn't dare die yet. He had a message to deliver and brothers to avenge. How would he face The One God should he fail in this most important mission?

The obvious answer was that he wouldn't. No doubt some hell dedicated to failures would welcome him with open arms.

When his horse reached the foot of the church steps, the sun had nearly set. Thankfully there was no service. Gaius had no desire to wade through several hundred members of the rich and powerful. Not that he ever did, but tonight especially their phony piety would grate on his weary nerves.

Focusing on putting one foot in front of the other, Gaius trudged up the steps, paused to make the circle over his heart, and pushed through the unlocked doors. A priest stood at the far end of the chapel, pale hair and skin marking him as a provincial. His white robes were spotless and his eyes appeared unshadowed.

Lucky bastard.

Gaius immediately banished the unworthy thought. The priests had their work to do and the White Knights had theirs. If someone had offered him a chance to trade his white cloak for the robes of a priest and easy duty in some church in the countryside, he'd refuse. Gaius made his choice the moment he felt called to fight for his faith. Nothing save a command from The One God himself, or maybe the pope, would be enough to get him to renounce his choice.

When Gaius had covered half the distance separating him

from the priest the other man bowed. "Welcome, Brother. What brings one of The One God's holy warriors to us at this hour?"

The priest's kind, gentle words made Gaius feel even worse about his earlier thoughts. "I have an important message for His Holiness. Please get word to him right away."

The priest's face paled. "His Holiness doesn't speak to the likes of me. I can relay any message to Cardinal Rufious, His Holiness's advisor. If he feels the matter warrants the pope's time, I'm sure he'll pass it along."

Gaius pulled out the medallion Cossus had given him. "Commander Cossus, my commanding officer, ordered me to present this medallion to His Holiness and deliver my message. I have been riding virtually nonstop for three weeks to get here. Tell that to whomever you have to, but I'm not leaving until I've had an audience."

The priest bowed for a second time. "Your determination to complete your superior's task does you great credit. I will speak with the cardinal and impress that upon him. The pews are not the most comfortable of places, but please, rest yourself. I know not how long it will take to get the cardinal's decision."

"The One God bless you, Father. Commander Cossus held great faith that the amulet would be known to those above us. If you use his name and describe it, you may get a reply faster than you fear." Gaius dropped into the nearest pew and failed to suppress a sigh of relief.

When he looked up again, the priest had gone.

———

There were days—more since his ill-fated decision to bring Joran Den Cade in for questioning—that Cardinal Rufious hated his job. Septimus had never been especially interested in doing the actual work of being pope. He liked the trappings and power. More importantly, he had the talent, when he chose to employ it, to project the church's authority in a way that made the rich and powerful both fearful and eager to donate. That skill sufficed to make all the extra work he created for Rufious worthwhile.

But lately he hadn't even been doing that and the church coffers showed it. All he did was whinge about the stolen holy sword and how it was an affront to the church and The One God himself. The fact that they had already acknowledged that The One God was only convenient fiction didn't seem to faze him or slow down the complaints.

All Rufious could do was nod and try to coax him back to doing his actual job. So far, his efforts had been mostly unsuccessful.

When the knock sounded on his door, Rufious looked up from the scroll he'd been reading with relief. That relief lasted just long enough for him to realize that no one would be visiting him at this hour unless there was a problem. And if there was one thing he didn't need, it was another problem.

Nevertheless he said, "Come in."

The door opened and a nervous, twitching priest inched inside. The youth—if he was a day over twenty-two Rufious would eat Septimus's new hat—looked everywhere but at him. He reminded Rufious of nothing so much as a mouse about to be introduced to the family cat.

"Calm down, man, and tell me what brings you from your post this evening."

"Yes, Your Eminence. A White Knight just arrived and demanded to speak with the pope. He says he has a message from a Commander Cossus and he has a gold medallion marked with the crimson circle of The One God. He seemed to think these two facts would mean something to you."

Rufious didn't hear anything after Cossus's name and the description of the medallion. Only a handful of people had one of those and the hero Cossus was one. If he gave it to someone else along with a message, it could only mean something world-shaking had happened.

"Where is this White Knight?" Rufious asked.

"In the chapel. He refused to leave without an answer, but I did convince him to at least sit down. Poor fellow looked about ready to fall over."

That only confirmed Rufious's fears. "I will speak with His Holiness and come to collect the knight shortly. Bring him food and drink that he might be refreshed before his interview."

The priest's eyes widened slightly. "You mean the pope will actually speak with him?"

"Oh yes. The bearer of that medallion will be granted an audience anytime, day or night. I would bring him at once only I want to give His Holiness time to prepare for the meeting." And make sure he's not passed out drunk or with the nuns. Rufious didn't think it wise to say that last bit out loud.

"I will see to our esteemed guest at once." The priest bowed and hurried away.

Rufious scrubbed a hand across his face. Had he ever been that young and idealistic? He doubted the latter for sure. Rufious came from a noble family of fairly high rank, so idealism had been beaten out of him at a very young age. Only cynicism and hypocrisy remained and that had served him very well in his current position.

With a long sigh that summed up his feelings far more eloquently than words ever could, Rufious pushed away from the desk and strode out of his office and down the hall that led to Septimus's private chambers. He didn't even consider checking the office. That room implied work and Septimus avoided anything even vaguely resembling work.

Rufious stopped in front of a closed wooden door engraved with an image of the church in front of The One God's circle. Three sharp knocks echoed in the hall.

Long minutes passed before the door squeaked open and a

pudgy, slightly bleary-eyed face stared up at him. The pope wore his sleeping robe open to the waist, giving an appallingly clear view of his less-than-divine physique. At least the stink of wine and spirits didn't make Rufious's eyes water. That was better than he'd expected.

"What?" the pope asked.

"A bearer of the Gold One amulet has arrived with a message. It's Cossus's."

Septimus shook his head and blinked a few times. "Refresh my memory."

"Cossus commands our easternmost fortress, the one with the demon artifact in the basement."

"Right. What's the message?"

"I don't know. The bearer has orders to deliver them to you and he seems the loyal and stubborn sort if the priest that met him is to be believed. Whatever's going on, if Cossus handed over the amulet, you can be certain it's nothing good."

"Fuck! I don't need this right now."

Rufious shared that sentiment wholeheartedly. "Unfortunately, whether we need it or not is irrelevant. I have to assume that time is of the essence, so if you'd get ready and head to your office, I'll go collect the messenger and meet you there."

"Fine. Where's my new hat?"

"I assume on the hat rack in your office. And Septimus, don't forget the mints."

His Holiness turned away and shuffled deeper into his room muttering about where Rufious could shove his mints.

Some days, today for example, Rufious seriously debated trying to find a job in the palace. Of course, they'd just assume he was a spy and send him on his way. No, he was stuck with the church and vice versa.

And if that wasn't enough to confirm to him that The One God didn't exist, nothing would.

———

"Sir?"

A distant voice tried to yank Gaius back to waking. Since he wanted few things less than to wake, Gaius ignored it.

"Sir?" This time the voice added a hesitant shake of his shoulder.

Since Florens never did anything hesitantly, it wasn't his commanding officer trying to wake him. That meant failing to respond wouldn't result in a boot to his backside. He needed no more encouragement to ignore whoever wanted him.

That's when the scent of something meaty and savory reached him. Gaius's mouth watered and his stomach immediately demanded that he open his eyes and find out where that smell came from.

"Sir?" the stubborn voice asked for the third time. "Cardinal Rufious commanded that I bring you a meal. Our stew is humble but filling. Won't you wake and eat before your audience with His Holiness?"

Everything came rushing back to Gaius then. Cossus, the message, all of it. His eyes snapped open and he sat up.

Where? Oh, right, the church in Tiber. He'd fallen asleep with his head on his arms in one of the pews.

His neck crunched as he turned to look at the nervous priest in white now burdened with a tray laden with a bowl of steaming stew and a chunk of brown bread.

Seeing that he had his wits somewhat about him, the priest held out the tray.

"Thank you." Gaius rested it on his lap and made the circle over his heart. "Will you sit with me, Father? I haven't eaten a meal with company in what seems ages. I'm Gaius."

"Lar." The priest settled in the next pew up from him. "You must have faced a perilous journey to arrive so exhausted."

"Long, but not so perilous. I fear I can offer you no details."

Gaius spooned some of the stew into his mouth and swallowed. Mutton cooked until tender. Very nice.

"Forgive me, I didn't mean to pry. When I saw Cardinal Rufious's reaction to your arrival, I just knew it had to be something exciting." Lar looked into the rafters with a faraway gaze. "I wanted to be a White Knight, out fighting to spread the faith, but I lacked the strength and temperament. The instructors said The One God needed my service here. They were just being polite. I would have made a terrible knight."

"We all serve Him as best we are able. If this is to be your place, give your all every day and He will favor you. At least that's what my commanding officer always said."

"Your commander sounds very wise."

Gaius found he had trouble swallowing the piece of bread in his mouth. When he finally got it down, he said, "He was."

Slow understanding spread across Lar's face and he fell silent. Much as he wanted company, Gaius found he now appreciated silence.

Fifteen minutes later, his meal now just a pleasant memory, Gaius spotted a crimson-robed cardinal emerge from a door behind the altar. He scrambled to his feet followed a moment later by a clearly confused Lar.

The priest turned and immediately bowed to the man in red. "Your Eminence, forgive me, I didn't hear you enter. Gaius, allow me to introduce His Eminence Cardinal Rufious, most noble advisor to His Holiness the Pope."

Gaius bowed as well though not as deeply as Lar. There were two sides to the church hierarchy, the martial side and the spiritual side. Though they all answered to the pope and Rufious ranked high enough that Gaius would have to be insane not to obey one of his orders, he still technically didn't answer to the cardinal. He would show respect, deference even, but he refused to do any more.

"Welcome, Knight Gaius." Rufious closed the distance

between them, stopping a few feet away. "The good father has told me some of your story. If Commander Cossus sent you, the situation to the east must be truly terrible."

"It is, Eminence." Gaius flicked a glance at Lar. "Do you wish to discuss it here or wait until we join His Holiness?"

"We will wait. The pope is getting ready for your audience and we'll go back to his office shortly. I wish to confirm Cossus's medallion before we go."

Gaius pulled it out of his tunic, lifted it over his head, and handed it to Rufious. The cardinal took only a moment to nod and offer it back. That came as a surprise. Gaius assumed he'd have to turn it over so the higher-ups could give it to some other, more worthy person.

"Thank you," Rufious said. "I've only seen one other medallion, which tells you how rare they are."

"Commander Cossus told me as much. Every knight knows his story, but hearing about the medallion really drives home how great a man he was."

Rufious shot him a sharp look and Gaius immediately realized his mistake. He'd just admitted to a low-ranking priest that one of the heroes of the order was dead. Stupid! It showed exactly how tired he'd gotten.

"Perhaps we should head back now. Should His Holiness need more time to ready himself, we can wait in his office. Excuse us, Father."

Lar bowed again. "I will return to my post."

Gaius fell in behind Rufious and they walked out of the chapel via the same door through which Rufious entered. A rather austere passage led deeper into the church than Gaius had ever gone. In fact, when he thought back, he hadn't even been past the chapel. Not that there was any reason for a low-ranking White Knight to have access to the back halls of the First Church. The highest of the high in the spiritual branch gathered here to work out exactly how best to spread the faith.

Once they made up their minds, the White Knights would be informed and make the plans necessary to carry them out in concert with the imperial army.

After what seemed like a long time, they stopped before a carved door. Rufious knocked and a stern voice said, "Enter."

Gaius found his mouth dry and tried to work up enough spit to swallow. Despite his confidence, he was about to stand in the presence of the most powerful man in the empire and The One God's representative. He found the prospect daunting.

Rufious reached for the handle, paused, and looked at him. "Take a breath. Stay calm. Deliver your message, answer our questions to the best of your ability, and you'll be fine. We all serve The One God and no mortal man, even the pope, is perfect. Keep these facts in mind and you'll be fine."

Gaius finally blew out a long sigh. "Thank you, Your Eminence. I'm okay now."

It surprised Gaius that he actually meant that. They were all brothers despite the difference in rank.

Beyond the door waited a remarkably mundane office. A man of average appearance dressed in a fine white robe sat behind a desk free of clutter or any other trappings you'd expect to find in an office. On a stand nearby rested a tall white hat marked with The One God's crimson circle.

Gaius offered a bow deep enough to show his full respect for the office and the man in it. "Holiness, I bear a message from Fortress Commander Cossus regarding a matter most dire."

"My most sincere thanks for completing the difficult journey to bring news from the east." The pope offered a warm, kind smile. "Please, make your report."

Gaius did so, sparing no detail of the attack and subsequent retreat. When he finished, he added, "The commander's plan was to hole up in the basement and hold out as long as possible. Given what I saw, I fear there's no hope for my brothers."

The pope tapped his chin, clearly deep in thought.

"What did the wizard leading them look like?" Rufious asked.

"I never got a clear look at him, or her, I suppose. All I saw was a figure in a dark cloak. There was a hint of a face that looked partially melted. No arrow could touch him and after he transformed the bile zombies into that spider thing, we had no hope of winning. It is my most fervent prayer that The One God sends him to the deepest, blackest pit in hell."

"So the wizard, his zombie minions, and the strange crow that attacked you after you escaped were the only foes you faced?" the pope asked.

"Yes, Holiness. Looking back, it seems like such a small force, yet we were defeated so easily."

"Never underestimate the power of the church's enemies," the pope said. "Were it within their power, many would see us laid low and our holy work put to ruin. But we won't allow them to have their way. Our fortress will be reclaimed and the wizard responsible for this insult dealt with."

Gaius bowed again. "I request permission to join the mission to retake the fortress. I owe my brothers that at least."

The pope offered a warm, fatherly smile. "Granted. Go now to the barracks and rest. Plans will be made and the emperor contacted. I know this is a church matter, but given the danger, we'll need the army's help, particularly in the form of extra dragon ships. You will be alerted before they're ready to depart."

"Thank you, Holiness."

Rufious touched his elbow. "I'll take you back to the chapel. Can you find your way to the barracks from there?"

"Yes, Eminence. I spent several weeks there before receiving my assignment to the east."

Gaius quickly found himself escorted out of the back halls and into the chapel where Father Lar remained standing vigil should any follower arrive in need.

The youthful priest smiled. "Did your meeting go well?"

"Very well, thank you, Father. His Holiness has a kind way about him. I had no idea what to expect, but he was everything I imagined the pope to be. Perhaps we will see each other again during my visit. Good evening."

Lar offered a shallow bow. "I would like that very much, Gaius."

Gaius staggered down the aisle and out into the cool evening air. An actual bed would be a delight beyond words. Somehow, he'd delivered Cossus's message. Whatever happened now was out of his hands.

―――

When Rufious made it back to Septimus's office, he opened the door without knocking and stared as soon as he stepped inside. Septimus had a book in his lap, his head down, working. He had to be dreaming.

Septimus looked up. "Don't just stand there like an idiot, come here and help me try and figure out what, exactly, we were hiding in that fortress."

Rufious strode over to the desk and stood beside Septimus. "Sorry. It's just been a long time since I saw you with a book in your hand."

Septimus snorted. "You know I wasn't always the pope. I used to work in the archive. Just because work is now beneath my position, doesn't mean I don't remember how to do it. This logbook is useless by the way. All it says is 'demonic artifact, purpose unknown.' Did we really build and staff that huge fortress in order to protect something whose purpose we don't understand?"

Rufious read the entry then said, "There's more on page sixty."

Septimus scowled up at him before looking down at the entry and muttering, "Stupid, know-it-all cardinal."

Rufious forced himself not to smile. The fortress's fall might end up a blessing in disguise if it served to get Septimus's mind focused on something other than the missing sword. He seemed more like his old self than he had in a long time.

The pope paged over to number sixty and they found a sketch of a black orb resting on a tripod of some sort. Underneath the image an entry said anyone touching the orb died instantly, making moving it an impossibility. The pope at the time had judged the artifact so dangerous that it warranted a fortress to keep it out of the hands of any evil force that might want to use it to harm the empire and its people.

"Well, we know what it does at least," Septimus said. "Maybe we'll get lucky and the wizard will touch it and kill himself, problem solved."

"Somehow I doubt a wizard powerful enough to take over our fortress doesn't know about the artifact and its dangers. I'd wager our enemy has some way to overcome that threat."

"You're probably right, damn you. I really am going to have to speak with Marcus, aren't I?"

"This does seem like the sort of thing the emperor should know about. If the danger should prove as grave as we fear, the White Knights likely won't be enough to deal with it on their own. We'll need the army to back us up."

"Fine, but not tonight. I'm too hungover."

"I can hardly tell."

Septimus shot him a venom-filled look. "Are you hoping for an assignment in the provinces?"

"Certainly not, Holiness." Rufious forced himself not to smile.

"I'll take a cure all and head over in the early afternoon tomorrow."

"Very good. I'll contact the palace and arrange a specific time."

Septimus nodded and Rufious started to leave. "What did you do with that far-too-earnest White Knight?"

Rufious turned back. "I sent him to the barracks to rest. When the expedition is sent to reclaim the fortress, he's the only one that's seen the wizard. I figure he'll be useful."

"Fine. Good night."

"Good night, Septimus."

Rufious really did leave this time. He needed to write a note to the palace. No, probably better if he went himself. A cardinal serving as messenger boy would get their attention better than anything he might write. Not to mention after everything they went through with that demon thing, Rufious had a standing invitation to see the crown prince anytime day or night should another emergency come up. He could, of course, just tell them what was happening on his own, but for political reasons, it would be best to let Septimus do that.

Given what he read about the demon artifact, it seemed these sorts of games should be set aside, but they never were. The church and the palace would be playing stupid political games even if the city were burning down.

Rufious dearly hoped it didn't come to that.

CHAPTER 20

Alexandra stalked through the halls of the palace toward her father's private meeting room. A pair of servants took one look at her and quickly ducked down a side passage. That had been happening a lot since Joran vanished. And that's all he did. Until someone showed her a body, Alexandra refused to believe he was dead. The universe wouldn't be so cruel as to let her meet a man she might actually be able to love only to take him away when she finally realized it.

She chuckled at her own naiveté. If she knew one thing for sure, it was that the universe didn't give a damn about her or anyone else despite the nobility's self-importance. No, whatever happened in her love life, she held no illusions about its importance in the grand scheme of things.

At least the pathetic sobbing had stopped. Now she just had anger issues such that the servants had trouble looking at her. That actually suited her persona as the Iron Princess better. If anyone saw her weeping into her pillow like a little girl, she'd never live it down.

Thankfully, one of the youths that served as a palace

messenger had come knocking on her door yesterday evening with a note saying that the pope would be joining them for an important meeting this afternoon.

That was it, no details, no nothing. Hopefully something important but not too disastrous had happened and she could throw herself into solving the problem. Any kind of distraction would be welcome.

She rounded a corner and nearly ran face-first into General Ventor, her second in the Iron Legion. He wore a fine crimson and silver tunic with the legion's sword on its chest.

He put his hands on her shoulders.

Alexandra shrugged him off. This was not the distraction she wanted. "Out of the way, Ventor, I'm on my way to see Father."

"Surely you can spare me a moment. I wanted to offer my most sincere condolence for the loss of your fiancé."

He all but smirked the words. If she hadn't been short of competent generals, Alexandra would have happily cut his head off and put it on a pike in front of the palace.

"Noted." She tried to step around him, but he moved to block her path.

"I'd be happy to offer you any comfort you might need. It is also my intention to ask His Imperial Majesty for the chance to court you." He put his hands on her shoulders again. "I think we'd make a good pair."

Alexandra brought her knee up into his groin.

Ventor groaned and slumped against the wall before sliding to the floor, his handsome face twisted in pain.

She crouched in front of him. "I don't need comforting from the likes of you. And Joran is missing, not dead. One last thing, Ventor. If you ever put your hands on me again without being asked, I'll have them cut off and burned."

"My hands?" He barely squeaked out the question.

"Yes, those too." Alexandra stood, turned on her heel, and stormed off.

Telling off Ventor made her feel better and she found the worst of her anger had cooled. Just as well as she'd need a clear head to deal with whatever emergency had popped up.

Five minutes later found her striding past a pair of imperial guards, both of whom touched fist to heart as she passed. Only a select few servants ever entered this part of the palace. The throne room was where public business happened, but almost anything really important got moved here, where only those that needed to know heard the details.

Another pair of guards stood on either side of a closed door engraved with the imperial lion. Without a word they opened it for her allowing her access to her father's private study.

Unlike the public areas of the palace with their gold and silk decorations, this room was all business. Father sat behind a plain, hardwood desk in a battered but comfortable leather chair. He did wear his crown along with a fine robe of crimson and gold.

"Father, what's the emergency?" she asked before sitting in the smaller chair beside him.

"I don't know any details," her father said. "Septimus's pet cardinal offered none when he arrived to make the arrangements for this meeting last night. He said it would be best if we discussed it directly with the pope. Stupid games, but I suppose we have appearances to keep up. Not that anyone's going to see down here."

"Where's Marcus? I assumed he'd be joining us if the situation is as bad as it sounds."

"Your brother had an engagement with some other nobles in regard to a boundary dispute between two barons. I pushed the job off on him. I'm sick of their complaints and if I had to listen to any more, I might have ordered them hung just to see if their sons are more reasonable."

"This isn't the same dispute that's been going on for like the last five months, is it?"

He nodded, looking tired. "Anyone that claims being emperor is exciting needs to spend an afternoon with those idiots. Hopefully Marcus has better luck. If he gets them to agree on something, anything, it will be worth however much brandy they drink in the process."

A dull thud sounded on the door.

"That will be Septimus." Father straightened, the role of emperor settling over him like a cloak. "Send them in."

The door opened and the pope entered, dressed in full regalia with Cardinal Rufious trailing along behind dressed in formal red robes. The pair made the short walk to Father's desk. The door clunked solidly shut. Some alchemical treatment absorbed sound so if you pressed your ear to the outside of the door you'd hear nothing.

Father raised a hand before either man had a chance to speak. "It's just the four of us. What say we cut through the formalities and get straight to the point. The good cardinal made it sound like the situation was grim."

Septimus doffed his ludicrous white hat and handed it to Rufious. "Grim is putting it mildly. An unknown wizard has seized control of one of our fortresses. This particular fortress protected an artifact of demonic origin. Other than killing anyone that made contact with it, we have no idea what it might be capable of. The messenger and sole-surviving White Knight of the garrison indicated that everyone else died in the attack. He didn't see it happen, but given the creature the wizard sent against them, he saw no path for them to survive."

Alexandra's mind raced. Wizards and artifacts were way outside her area of expertise. Of all the times for Joran to be missing.

Father leaned forward in his chair. "Is this another of the secrets you didn't feel the need to share with the Crown?"

"The fortress and artifact have been secure for centuries. I had only passing knowledge of it. If one of my predecessors told one of yours, I have no idea. Much like the secret of The One God, it may have been lost to time. Does it actually matter at this point?"

"No, I suppose it doesn't. What do you want from the Crown?"

"Soldiers and alchemists," Rufious said. As usual the cardinal had a better grasp of the details. "Given the report we received regarding the wizard's power, I doubt our White Knights have the numbers to get the job done on their own. A dragon ship to get the initial force there quickly would also be welcome."

"Where, exactly, is your fortress?" Alexandra asked.

"To the east, about ten miles from the ocean. Marching would take a month."

Father looked up at her. "Well?"

"The Fourth Legion is deployed in that general area. I'll send birds with orders for them to muster as quickly as possible. We have dragon ships in Tiber. If you can provide the White Knights, we have alchemists ready to depart at short notice."

"We can spare two hundred from the Tiber garrison," Rufious said. "Shall we meet at the landing field at first light?"

"That's fine. Do you have a map I can send to the Fourth?"

Rufious reached into an inside pocket and pulled out a scroll. "As it happens, I do."

Alexandra took the scroll and nodded her thanks. "I'll see you in the morning."

"Are there any other secrets you'd like to share, Septimus?" Father asked. "Anything that might bite us in the ass six months from now? Think hard. The next time you need help, the door might be locked."

Septimus snorted. "We all have our secrets, Marcus. At the end of the day, what's good for the church is good for the empire and vice versa. If we need help, you'll open the door.

Not because you want to help, but because you have to. You know it and so do I, so stop posturing."

A small, bitter smile curled Father's lip. "I think our meeting is over. Good afternoon, Holiness."

Septimus sketched a shallow, insulting bow. "Good afternoon, Your Imperial Majesty."

When the pope and cardinal had made their exit, Father said, "I hate that man. I hated him even when I thought he represented The One God on our world and now I think I hate him more. I wish that demon thing had killed him instead of my guards."

"I doubt anyone especially likes Septimus, but if he'd gotten killed, we might have ended up with someone worse."

"I refuse to consider the possibility that such a person exists. How many alchemists will you send?"

"I can spare twenty without reducing the effectiveness of the First or Second. I'll make sure the dragon ship has a full load of alchemist's fire as well. For now, I need to get ready. If you'll excuse me, Father."

"You're not going. Make whatever arrangements you need to, but you are not going yourself." Father shot her his best "don't question me on this" glare. "Is that clear?"

"It is, but this is exactly the sort of emergency the Iron Princess should handle."

"No. If they fail, and I can't imagine an entire legion plus the advance team falling to a single wizard and his monster, then it will be your responsibility to clean up the mess. We are not having a debate, Alexandra. Defy me and I swear I'll find a new supreme commander of the army."

"You won't find anyone as good at it as I am. For the well-being of the empire, the job is mine until I'm dead." She raised a hand, cutting off his protest. "I won't argue on this mission. Leading White Knights isn't something I'm interested in doing and General Amelious is talented enough to handle the Fourth regardless of the challenge. I'll dispatch their orders then get to work on plans should they all fail."

"That's my girl." Father cleared his throat. "About Joran—"

"He's missing, not dead, at least until I see a body. Ventor's making noises about courting me."

"Ha! I don't need to cultivate his family's support. They're already completely devoted to the empire. Marrying you off to him would be a complete waste. Besides, even by noble standards he's an arrogant shitheel. I can't imagine having to eat dinner with him on a regular basis."

"You wouldn't have to. If you marry me off to him, Ventor won't survive the honeymoon." She kissed his cheek. "I need to get to work. How about breakfast with Marcus tomorrow after I get the dragon ship off?"

Father nodded. "That sounds nice. We'll meet in the garden."

Alexandra smiled and took her leave. Her smile lasted until she was out of sight of the guards. She hated it when Father got overprotective. Not that he was wrong. Against a regular army or even an insurgent force like the lizardmen, she had no doubt about her ability to deal with them, but when it came to magic, she felt totally out of her depth.

By The One God, she wished Joran were here.

CHAPTER 21

Ten more days of walking had largely depleted their supply of preserved meat. The starchy vegetables were long gone and only a rare rain shower allowed them to top off their water skins. All in all, when the six black towers that Joran assumed marked their destination appeared in the distance, he couldn't have been happier. Hopefully this bile portal activated as easily as the one that brought them here.

He reached into his pocket and ran his thumb over the slightly rough surface of the black pearl Grub took from Samaritan. Would it activate this portal as easily as Samaritan's did the other? He dearly wanted that to be so. Bahesti had been a fine guide, but depending on the metal man for everything did nothing to put Joran's mind at ease.

Oddly, after their meeting with the angel, Mia's anxiety seemed to have lessened. When he asked her about it one night by the fire, she said knowing there were beings like him out there watching over them made her feel secure in a way she hadn't since the pope admitted The One God was a lie. He was glad for her and wished he felt the same way himself. When he thought about angels his mind went automatically to how they planned to use humans to further their plans. Having met the angel and felt the... goodness about him, for lack of a better word, Joran understood that whatever the angel did would be done for the best possible reason. Unfortunately, being used for a good reason made him feel no better than being used for a bad reason.

"What the hell was this place?" Grub asked as they drew closer to the cluster of towers.

Joran couldn't deny his own curiosity. Unlike Bahesti's village, this didn't look like a city. The towers were shorter, smaller, and spaced too close together. He guessed they covered half a mile at most.

"This is, or was, an experimental facility. Teams of wizards came to access the bile spring and use its power to perform whatever ritual they had in mind. I believe the prototypes for the giant beasts Joran encountered were first made here."

"Generous of the overmages to let their underlings have access to something so useful," Joran said, not believing for a moment that the lords of this land did anything for anyone's sake save their own.

"Oh, there was a price. Any wizard that wanted access had to submit all the details of their spell ahead of time."

"So the overmages could deny access for projects they disapproved of. Not to mention stealing anything that caught their interest." Joran nodded. "A good system, for them anyway."

"Every system in the Black Iron Empire was good for the overmages. If it wasn't, they outlawed or destroyed it."

They topped a small hill and the little group came to a halt. At the edge of a shallow depression about a mile across jutted the towers. Like everything else in the ruined empire, the land was black and dead. Joran had expected to find buildings or something where the wizards worked, but other than the towers, there was nothing.

"Did the wizards conduct their experiments in the towers?" Joran asked.

"No, the towers served as anchors for the wards that kept any out-of-control magic from damaging the surrounding land." Bahesti gave a sad shake of his head. "The protections have long since failed. The labs and workshops are underground and thus closer to the bile spring. The portal chamber is adjacent to the spring. Since wizards were constantly coming and going, there were no fixed wards here."

"How do we access the underground complex?" Joran asked.

"That may be trickier. The dragon's attack caused tremendous earthquakes that tore the land apart, as you've seen. While the complex itself was well built and should have survived with minimal damage, it appears that the entry has collapsed."

"Marvelous." Joran turned to Grub. "Any chance your magic can confirm the underground chambers survived? Not much point digging them out if nothing's left to find."

"Sure it can, that's what geomancers train for. But it'll be a lot easier if we're closer."

Since nothing indicated danger, they set out down the hill. Joran felt no different when they passed between the two nearest towers. He risked a glance at the ether and confirmed that no magic crackled around them. Nothing in the clearing concerned him either. As far as he could tell they were alone in the world.

"Is it me, or does this place give you the creeps?" Mia asked. "It feels like horrible things happened here."

"I suspect horrible things happened everywhere in this broken land." Joran reached out and squeezed her free hand. "But likely more happened here than usual. Are you okay?"

She nodded. "I'll be glad to get home."

"You and me both." Grub had the mithril amulet out and was no doubt doing something magical. Joran didn't bother to look.

Without an explanation it would be meaningless to him. "What will you have the palace chef prepare when we get back?"

"Something with lots of gravy. I'm sick of dried meat."

Joran grinned. "Maybe we should visit my parents instead. Their chef makes the best stew."

She smiled back. "Good idea. We can bring the princess, that way your mom won't have to talk to me."

"Looks like everything underground is intact," Grub said, interrupting their pleasant musings.

"I found the collapsed entrance," Stoneheart called from a few yards away. "I'd guess an hour to dig it out."

"My golem can handle that," Bahesti said. "Another collapse won't hurt it."

No one objected and a few seconds later the golem got to work flinging dirt and rocks out of the entry tunnel. It finally felt like something was going their way.

———

Samaritan had never been so tired. He'd run out of wine a day ago and food two days before that. For some reason Overmage seemed even more obsessed with reaching their destination, sometimes refusing to stop for more than a few hours every night. Pointing out that he wasn't made of iron did little beyond slowing his relentless pace a fraction. Samaritan suspected that if he'd fallen behind, Overmage would have left him behind without a second thought.

Some partner.

Gomo kept up without issue, though he seemed rather amused by Samaritan's struggles. Of course, the red-skinned dwarf was a demon, so the suffering of mortals was no doubt his preferred form of entertainment.

"The towers at last." Overmage pointed ahead of them as if

Samaritan hadn't already noticed the six black towers sticking up into the air.

"Thank the universe for small favors," Samaritan said. "I assume you know how to activate the portal?"

"Of course I do," Overmage said in a tone that filled Samaritan with doubt.

They climbed a ridge and Overmage stopped so fast that Samaritan nearly slammed into his back. He peeked around and swore in a way that would have gotten him in deep trouble with his former comrades. In the low space between the towers, his hunters, along with a figure made of black iron, watched a second metal man, a golem Samaritan assumed, dig out a hole.

"How did they find this place much less get here ahead of us?" he asked.

No one had an answer of course. Doubtless Samaritan's rotten luck had something to do with it.

"We should go down there and kill them all," Overmage said. "This place belongs to the overmages and since I'm the last, it's mine. They're trespassing."

"I haven't rent mortal flesh in a while," Gomo said. "Just say when."

"How about we let them finish digging out the entrance then attack?" Samaritan suggested.

Overmage nodded. "Good idea. That's a job for commoners anyway."

Samaritan slumped to the ground and lay flat. If there was going to be a fight, he needed all the rest he could get.

———

Joran watched, toe tapping, as the golem slowly worked its way deeper into the ground. It had reached waist deep and the entrance showed no sign of opening up. Even though he knew it was going far faster than a human could, the progress seemed painfully slow. Having the end of his nightmare in sight no doubt played a part in his impatience. What he wouldn't have given for a shovel right now.

He touched his kit. During the journey here, he'd read the journal he took from the citadel library. He needed to confirm a few things in Tiber, but felt certain he knew about where the dragon slept. Finding the exact location would be difficult, but given the alternative, Joran figured they'd manage.

He clenched his jaw and immediately forced himself to relax. They needed to get back and the sooner the better.

None of the others seemed to share his anxiety. The dwarves were doing what they could to help with the digging, which amounted to little more than moving the piles of dirt out of the way so they didn't fall back into the hole. Bahesti, with his metal face, never gave any hint of his emotions.

As if summoned by his thoughts, Mia touched Joran's shoulder and whispered, "I think we're being watched."

Joran forced himself to be calm. Not now. Not when they were so close.

"Are you sure?"

"I saw a flash of white moving through the trees to the west. In this place, that has to be something unnatural."

"Samaritan."

As soon as Joran said the name, he knew it had to be true. Somehow the idea that they might escape without seeing him again never really occurred to Joran. His arrival seemed like destiny.

"And he's not alone. I caught glimpses of at least two others."

"Who would be crazy enough to work with that madman?" Joran immediately dismissed the irrelevant question. "How do you think we should handle it?"

Mia chewed her lip. "If we didn't need to control this location, I'd say we break into two groups, swing around and pincer them. Unfortunately, my guess is they want the portal as badly as we do. That means we hold here and make them come to us. If we get lucky, maybe we can retreat underground and fight them in a narrow passage. The problem is, I have no idea what the other two can do which makes it hard to plan."

"That's okay. I'll talk to Bahesti, you let the dwarves know. At least everyone will be ready when they attack."

Mia sent him a burst of reassurance and Joran returned it. With his soulmate by his side, he felt certain there was nothing beyond their ability to handle.

Joran left Mia's side and strolled over to Bahesti, who stood a few feet from the golem watching it scoop dirt with its hands.

The metal man looked up and cocked his head. "Is all well?"

Joran smiled and said, "We're being watched. An enemy of ours as well as at least two unknown parties. I don't know what they intend, but you can be sure it won't be good. I wanted you to be ready."

"Thank you for the warning. If they haven't attacked by now, I have to assume they plan to wait until we reach the underground workshop."

"That seems reasonable, but making assumptions can be dangerous. Best to just stay alert."

"Never fear; given my current circumstances, I'm always alert."

Joran nodded and flicked a glance at Mia. Stoneheart and Grub both looked calm, but she had to have told them by now. Well, he should've expected a soldier and a spy to have sufficient control of their emotions to give nothing away. When Mia finished talking with them he caught Grub's eye and nodded off to one side.

The dwarf joined him and Joran asked, "How much further?"

"Three or four feet plus however long the golem needs to make it wide enough for us to descend. Say four hours minimum."

"Thanks. I'd ask you to spy on Samaritan and his new friends, but I don't want them to know we're on to them."

"Smart. Samaritan might be insane, but he's not stupid. He'll be checking the ether from time to time just to be safe."

"Like you are?"

Grub smiled. "I'm not stupid either."

Joran wiped his forehead. Luckily it was hot enough that anyone watching would think his sweat came from the temperature rather than nerves. He really wasn't looking forward to another fight, but if they could kill Samaritan here, the threat of the dragon would be vastly reduced, at least for now.

For that, Joran would risk almost anything.

CHAPTER 22

Overmage looked down at the sleeping form of his human partner. Pathetic creatures, but useful in a way. There were limits on what he could do in his current body and having a flesh-and-blood human along should be useful. The other partner Samaritan mentioned also intrigued Overmage. A powerful wizard would make his task far easier. Unfortunately, as he well knew, powerful wizards were terribly difficult to control.

A soft growl drew his attention to the red-skinned demon staring down at the clearing below. Speaking of difficult things to control, unbound demons fell into that category as well. Gomo, as he called himself, had yet to prove as useful to the project as he claimed he would be. Not that Overmage doubted his power. Underestimating demons was a good way to end up dead or destroyed as the case may be.

"They have to be just about done," Gomo said. "Why don't we just attack now and be finished with them? The human can sleep through the battle and when we're done, we can wake him up. He'll just be in the way otherwise."

Overmage considered the demon's suggestion for a moment

then glanced down at the site. The enemy's golem had dug itself down over waist deep. It did seem likely that they had nearly cleared the entrance. Attacking before they finished would deny them an easy avenue of escape.

"Agreed. Do you have a plan?"

"I'm going to lead with a fireball then wade in and tear them limb from limb. You and your golem are welcome to help. Neutralizing their metal men would be a good start."

"Very well, leave those two to me. Are you certain you can handle the other four?"

"The day I can't handle four mortals is the day I give up my place in the forges. We strike on three."

Overmage nodded and with a mental command had his golem move to his side.

"Three... Two... One." Corrupt ether gathered around Gomo's hand and took on the shape of flames tinged with darkness.

His hand shot forward and the fireball rushed toward the clearing.

The battle would be over before it started.

———

"Magic incoming!" Grub's shouted warning sent Joran running toward the hole the golem had dug. Staying out of the fighters' way would be his most important task. If he saw a chance to take out Samaritan, so much the better.

He skidded to a stop beside the four-foot-deep hole and spun in time to see Grub, mithril amulet in hand, lash out with a spell that sliced an incoming fireball in half. The two pieces of the spell spun off to the left and right before exploding in bursts of reddish-black flames.

Definitely a good thing that didn't hit them.

"Our enemies have a demon with them," Bahesti said in a remarkably calm tone.

Joran had to remind himself that the metal man wanted to die and he probably didn't especially care who did the job. "How do you know?"

"Nothing else would be able to use the corrupted ether so well. At least nothing living in this ruined land. Here they come."

Three figures came sprinting down from the ridge where Mia first spotted them. One looked very much like Bahesti and another could have been a twin to his golem. The final member of the trio had to be the demon. It had red skin, stood about four feet tall, and appeared to have skinned a porcupine and glued the hide to his chin in place of a beard. The demon dwarf might have been a comical sight if not for the muscles rippling under his skin and a sword made of flames clutched in his right hand. Of Samaritan Joran saw no sign.

Bahesti crooked a finger and his golem climbed out of the hole. The pair walked over beside Mia, who had her sword drawn, ready to cut down anyone that got close.

The others were much more qualified to handle the enemies bearing down on them. Joran shifted his attention to the hole behind him. He pulled out a blue light, shook it, and lay down for a closer look.

A thunderous impact shook the clearing.

Sounded like the battle had begun.

Forcing himself to ignore everything else, Joran extended his arm as far as it would go. A stone tunnel was visible at the bottom of the hole. The golem had actually broken through. The opening would be a tight fit for the dwarves with their broad shoulders, but if they forced it, Joran figured everyone would be able to get through.

If the worst happened, at least they had an escape route.

M ia clutched her mithril sword, planted her feet, and waited for the red-skinned dwarf thing to close the distance between them. Even from a distance she felt the wrongness of the creature. Its presence felt exactly the opposite of the angel's gentle warmth. That was how she knew it had to be a demon, albeit a different sort of demon from the one she fought in the palace.

Horrible as it was, this one appeared solid and she preferred that to one capable of turning to smoke at the drop of a hat. She should be able to fight it without Joran having to exhaust himself helping her. In fact, she felt him, calm and safe, behind her. She needed no more incentive to stop these monsters here and now.

"I'll handle my confused fellows if you deal with the demon." Mia had been so focused on the approaching threat that she didn't even notice Bahesti come up behind her. Under other circumstances that might have been a fatal mistake.

She flicked a glance at him as their enemies reached the flat area directly ahead. "You're not going to have a problem fighting one of your own people?"

"Under other circumstances, maybe, but not with this opponent. Rest assured I will not hesitate to do what I must."

Mia felt better, not that she had much choice. Dealing with the demon would take all of her concentration.

She shifted a bit to the right so they'd both have room to fight.

Ten feet from her the demon roared and leapt.

Mia spun and countered with a sweeping left-to-right uppercut slash.

When her sword made contact the demon's sword wavered, flickered, and tried to vanish.

It snarled and jumped back. "A mithril sword, damn the luck.

Of all the things I thought to find in this wretched hole, that wasn't one of them."

Mia lunged without a word.

Her sword passed through air as the demon vanished only to reappear ten feet to her left, its sword back to full power.

She snarled her annoyance. This one could disappear too, just in a different way. Was that something all demons did, or only the ones she ran into?

Mia had no more time to think about it.

The demon threw its fire sword at her like a spear.

She slashed it in half and the flames vanished without burning her. Her sword, at least, worked as good against this thing as the last one.

Now she just had to get close enough to kill it.

They dodged around each other, neither gaining an advantage. The demon used its disappearing trick to evade her sword and Mia simply cut apart any magic it sent her way.

She badly wanted to close and it badly didn't want to let her. Its reluctance to fight close quarters made it clear the demon feared her sword and that gave Mia even greater confidence. But what she really needed was a break.

That break arrived seconds later. The demon tried to jump back when she charged.

When it did, a lightning bolt shot in, striking it full in the chest.

It froze for a heartbeat and that was all the opening Mia needed.

She swung hard, determined to remove its head once and for all.

Somehow the demon recovered enough to raise an arm.

Mia sliced it off at the elbow, but that slowed her blade enough for the demon to vanish again. This time it didn't reappear where she could see it. Though she knew the thing wasn't dead, for now at least it seemed their battle was over.

Flicking what little demon blood hadn't burned off her sword to the ground, she turned to thank Grub for his help. She caught a flash of white before Samaritan did to Grub what she had just done to the demon.

She hurried over, but Samaritan fled as fast as his legs could carry him.

Grimacing at the stump of Grub's right arm, she pulled the belt out of his pants and twisted it around the severed wrist.

She already sensed Joran coming. If anyone could save Grub, he could.

———

When the first explosion sounded Samaritan sat bolt upright. He stared at the leaden sky for a moment trying to remember where he was. A tremendous crash of metal on metal reminded him. The Black Iron Empire, trying to get home. From the sounds of it, his so-called allies had started the battle without him. That didn't especially surprise him given Overmage's arrogance and Gomo's power. They probably figured he'd just be in the way.

And maybe they were right.

Samaritan scrambled to his feet and turned to see Overmage chatting with another metal man while two nearly identical golems wrestled around a few feet away. Gomo battled the woman that stole his amulet and as far as he could tell they were at a stalemate.

He caught a glimpse of Grub and his heart skipped a beat. The dwarf held his amulet. Samaritan needed to get it back. If he could contact the archbishop, she might be able to open a portal of her own, sparing him the need to seize control of the bile portal. Of course, that was a big "might" and he still hoped to keep his options open.

Regardless, he wanted his amulet back and killing the traitor wouldn't hurt his feelings any either.

Samaritan drew his sword and circled around to approach the dwarf from behind. A fair fight with a wizard, even one as weak as Grub, didn't overly interest him.

At least the clanging of the golems provided noise to cover his approach. He hurried to get into position before the fight ended.

A minute later he stood directly behind Grub. A quick glance into the ether revealed a rapidly gathering spell forming around the dwarf's hand.

Perfect.

When a wizard released a spell, it took every ounce of concentration. There was no better moment to strike.

Despite the pain, Samaritan kept his sight shifted to view the ether. When Grub's targeting thread shot out, he charged.

The lightning bolt lanced out, sending spots dancing in front of Samaritan's eyes.

Grub must have sensed him approaching.

The dwarf shifted at the last moment. With his vision still blurry, Samaritan had no hope of changing the angle of his sword.

Instead of taking Grub in the neck, he hacked off the hand holding his amulet.

Grub collapsed.

Samaritan collected his prize and sprinted away. Let the traitor bleed to death, he didn't care. The amulet was what mattered most. Now that he had it again, he was content to let the others fight or flee as they preferred.

When he made it back to their lookout post, he found Gomo, one arm missing, standing further down the hill out of sight. Samaritan scuffed and skidded his way to the bottom and stopped beside the demon.

"Get that mithril away from me," Gomo said. "I've had enough of it for one day."

Samaritan's face twisted in confusion. "You mean the amulet? It's silver."

"No, it's mithril, the same as that bitch's sword. It purifies corruption and is poison to demons and undead. Can't you feel the difference when you hold it?"

Samaritan frowned. He'd been too busy running to think about it, but now that Gomo drew his attention to it, the air did feel lighter. When he shifted his vision there was no pain and the ether around him appeared devoid of the black threads he associated with corruption.

"Remarkable."

"Yeah, now put it away or get yourself away from me."

Samaritan pocketed the amulet and raised an eyebrow. "Better?"

"A little. Where's the arrogant statue? Hopefully carved into about a dozen pieces."

"Last I saw, he was chatting with the enemy's statue while their golems wrestled around doing no noticeable damage to each other. Will that heal?"

Gomo nodded and held up the stump. "In a few weeks. It's already stopped bleeding. Never figured I'd run into someone with a mithril sword in this corrupt shithole. I'm not going to fight her again."

"I thought you wanted to get back to Hell? If she kills you, won't that do the trick?"

"If a demon is killed by a mithril sword, our essence is purified. We can't return to Hell. Instead we'll dissipate into the ether as if we never were. If I were a mindless thrall, I wouldn't care, but I've lived for thousands of years and have no desire to end my eternal existence in this place."

Samaritan couldn't fault him for that. "What say we put some distance between us and them and I contact the archbishop. She might be able to bring us to her without a bile portal."

"You had me at 'put some distance between us and that sword.' Let Overmage catch up if he can."

Samaritan smiled, unsurprised by the demon's lack of loyalty. He'd hated Overmage since they first met.

The pair set off, both eager to put as much distance between themselves and the enemy as possible.

———

B ahesti stood, arms crossed, his golem at his side, and watched as another imperial citizen unlucky enough to survive the dragon's wrath ran toward him. If this was one of the dragon worshippers, conversation would be pointless, but he would try. Though he had no qualms about dealing with one of his fellows, he'd still prefer to avoid killing one of the few survivors.

He'd have smiled had his new body allowed it. As a man looking to die, he was hardly one to talk about the survival of their people.

The master stopped ten feet away while his golem kept charging.

Bahesti's own golem took two steps and swung a right cross that crashed into the enemy golem's face and sent it flying. The two automatons moved away, battering each other with their metal fists and doing precious little damage. He ordered his golem to keep the other one a safe distance away and turned his attention to the master.

"I don't suppose we can come to a peaceful solution?" Bahesti asked.

"We can," the stranger said. "Kneel before me and pledge your obedience to the last surviving overmage and I will allow you to continue existing."

Bahesti threw back his head and laughed. As soon as he heard the other's voice, he knew exactly what he dealt with. It wasn't another citizen at all. "You, an overmage? Don't be ridiculous. You're a citadel defense automaton. You were made to oversee the defenses of one of the overmage's citadels. Did your magical programing get scrambled when the dragon attacked? Clearly something's gone wrong with you."

The automaton twitched and shuddered, its head snapping left and right as if it might go flying right off. Bahesti couldn't begin to imagine what had happened to it. Perhaps the huge influx of corruption during the dragon's attack had severed some of its logic connections.

It gave one final shudder then stared at Bahesti again. "I am the last overmage. Kneel before your master and I will allow you to serve me."

Back to that again. "I don't think I will and our golems appear equally matched. What do you intend to do now?"

"Brawling is beneath me." The automaton nodded toward Mia and the demon. "Our servants can settle it. When my demon kills your swordswoman, you will be the next to fall. Unless you kneel and pledge your allegiance to your proper master."

Clearly the automaton had reached the limits of its broken logic spell. It was actually kind of sad. Of course it would be even sadder if the broken piece of trash wasn't getting in his way.

A howl of pain drew their attention to the other fight. Bahesti looked just in time to see the demon's arm hit the ground as it vanished. He'd never doubted Mia's chances of victory, especially after seeing her deal with the hyenataurs.

"It seems you're out of allies," Bahesti said. "She'll be along shortly to put you out of your misery."

The automaton shuddered and twitched. "No one defies an overmage and lives. You will suffer for this humiliation."

It turned and stomped away. The golem under its control tried to get away, but Bahesti's own golem had the superior position and refused to let it get up. He'd have Mia put it down shortly. If they had the misfortune to fight the automaton and its companion again, he'd prefer not to have to worry about the golem.

"Mia?" He found the woman kneeling beside Grub, who was also missing a hand.

It seemed their side hadn't come away unscathed after all.

———

J oran's head snapped up as soon as he felt Mia's fear. He and Stoneheart had been attempting to widen the tunnel entrance. The centurion, despite his considerable combat skills, had no weapon capable of harming either a demon or a person made of black iron. Annoyance at his powerlessness twisted the dwarf's face, but facts were facts.

Across the clearing he spotted Mia kneeling beside Grub. Whatever happened to the geomancer had to be the source of her disquiet since he felt no pain from her. Whatever happened, he needed to check it out. All signs of battle had ceased, so it should be safe enough.

He scrambled up and out of the hole, leaving his blue light behind. Stoneheart fell in beside him as they hurried over to Mia. What they found didn't look good. Grub lay on his back, Mia's makeshift tourniquet wrapped around his wrist. Someone had hacked his right hand off and there was no sign of the amulet.

"It was Samaritan," Mia said in answer to his unasked question.

No surprise there. Joran unslung his kit, pulled out the troll's blood paste, and applied a thick coat to the stump of Grub's arm. The last of the bleeding stopped at once.

After another half a minute Joran said, "You can loosen that."

Mia eased the tourniquet off and no blood gushed out. Good, the wound was fully sealed at least.

"Don't worry," Joran said. "We'll get you a cure all as soon as we reach the capital. That hand will grow back in no time."

Grub growled in the back of his throat. "My own damn fault. I was so focused on the demon I lost all awareness of my surroundings. Bloody rookie mistake."

"Demons are very distracting," Joran said. "Don't beat yourself up. I think we've got the entrance opened up enough for everyone to fit through. If you're strong enough to stand, I'd just as soon get out of here before they decide to come back."

"I doubt they will, not after the thrashing they took." Joran looked up to see Bahesti approaching. "I was hoping I could prevail upon the young lady to finish off the enemy golem. Mine has it pinned down, but I'd prefer a more permanent solution."

Mia looked at him and Joran nodded. "Go ahead, we're all set here."

Joran stood and Stoneheart helped Grub up without being asked, a small kindness that surprised and pleased Joran. Perhaps losing an extremity in the line of duty finally proved to the stubborn centurion that Grub really was on their side.

A soft thunk prompted Joran to look Mia's way. She'd sliced the enemy golem's head off and now it lay still under Bahesti's. One threat eliminated at least. Joran dearly wished it had been Samaritan lying there instead, but he was proving terribly hard to kill.

And until he was dead, the danger of him waking the dragon remained.

"Time to go home." Joran's words were greeted with weary but eager smiles. Smiles that no doubted matched the one on his own face.

CHAPTER 23

Having spent most of the evening and night studying maps and sending messages to the Fourth, it was an exceedingly weary Alexandra that showed up at first light to meet Cardinal Rufious at the dragon ships' landing zone. The Iron Guards flanking her had the good sense to keep quiet and she and her slowly growing headache appreciated that.

When she arrived, White Knights were already marching up the loading ramps of the dragon ship she'd assigned to the mission. When it was gone, the available fleet would be reduced to two—Father's personal transport and the one she and Joran arrived in what seemed like a long time ago but was actually only a few months.

The dragon shipyards were busy working on three more to replace what they'd lost in Stello Province, but it took nearly a year to build a new dragon ship, so she wasn't counting on them to be of any help in the current crisis.

She spotted a man in crimson and angled that way. Alexandra found some bitter amusement in the fact that Rufious looked even more tired than she did. Working for the pope, especially a pope like Septimus, had to be one of the more exhausting jobs in the empire.

He offered a weary bow. "Good morning, Princess. The White Knights have their orders and are ready to depart as soon as they finish loading. I found your alchemists waiting so there should be no need to delay."

"Agreed. I sent orders to the Fourth. They'll march as soon as they get organized. I recommend your people play it safe until the legion gets there."

Rufious's smile held nothing of humor. "That's not the way of White Knights. Their brothers were wiped out and they'll be eager for retribution. I've told the knight commander to use his best judgement. How good that judgement will be, I have no idea."

"I guess we'll both have to pray." They shared a knowing look and Alexandra added, "Is there anything else you need from the Crown?"

"I don't believe so. Thank you for the loan of the ship."

"We're all in this together, Eminence. May The One God watch over us all."

"So say we all." He gave the ritual response and made a circle over his heart as if he actually meant it. Years of practice no doubt helped. "I need to return to the church, but I'll stay in touch."

"I'll let Father know the team has departed."

They exchanged nods of respect and Alexandra turned for the palace, pleased to have the formalities taken care of. She had always hated this part of her duties and tended to put them off on underlings, but right now she didn't trust Ventor not to undermine her at every opportunity.

Speaking of her obnoxious underling, it might be time to have him reassigned. She had other competent commanders she could elevate to general and she trusted them all more than Ventor even if they lacked his pure talent with command.

She swallowed a sigh and rubbed the bridge of her nose. Why did all the problems, big and small, seem to crop up at the same time?

Alexandra didn't know but when the crisis was over, she intended to sleep for a week, assuming she survived.

———

F ane nearly threw a very rare and valuable tome across her library. Her frustration had been growing by the hour and now it took all her considerable self-control not to blow something up. All her searching had come to nothing. There was no information on the artifact she found in the fortress. Nothing about a magical item capable of emitting that much corruption that also only destroyed beings of corruption while sparing normal humans.

Her master might know something about it, but she had no way to contact Lord Sur. And even he, genius that he was, might not have heard of such a thing. Its existence seemed utterly impossible to her, yet she'd seen and felt the results of its power firsthand.

Setting the book back in its place with exaggerated care, Fane allowed herself a deep breath and long sigh. Her undead body didn't get tired, but she did get mentally weary. Time for a break. She'd suck the life out of one of the prisoners, that should restore her focus. Scores of books remained unchecked in her library. Just because the obvious ones failed to yield the knowledge she wanted didn't mean one of the others wouldn't.

She took a step toward the door then froze when a familiar, distant tingle appeared in the back of her mind. It felt so distant she almost thought she imagined it at first. When it didn't go away, she hurried to her casting chamber. Such a weak connection would require her scrying sphere to complete.

A minute later she stood before the crystal orb and rested

her fingers on the cool, smooth surface. She sent ether into it and back out along the weak link, strengthening it as she went.

At last she reached the far end and found a surprise waiting. Samaritan, still alive, and holding his amulet in the bleakest environment she'd ever seen. Even through the weak link she sensed the amount of corruption surrounding him. If she didn't know better, Fane would have thought he'd ended up in Hell. He even had a one-armed demon nearby to strengthen the impression.

"I thought you were dead," she said at last.

"Not yet, though there have been several near scrapes. I lost my amulet for a time, that's why I haven't contacted you before now."

"That was my second guess. Where are you and how fares the mission?"

"I'm in what remains of the Black Iron Empire." Samaritan went on to tell her everything that had happened since he vanished from under the mountains. "Anyway, there's supposed to be an artifact that can lead us to the dragon. If you can portal us back, I believe we should have little trouble locating it."

Fane's excitement had grown while Samaritan spoke and now she practically quivered. That was the artifact's purpose. The corruption-destroying effects must be to prevent anyone from using it to find the dragon. Even better, as an ordinary human, Samaritan would have no trouble claiming it and leading her to the beast.

"I can do you one better. I believe I've already located the artifact you mentioned. Bringing you back will be no problem, but first, did you find the capital?"

"It's been destroyed and sunk to the bottom of the ocean by the dragon. There's nothing to find. However, I did find a library that held many fascinating texts. Whether they hold the secret of creating giant beasts or not, I can't say."

Fane let her pleasure ooze through the connection. "You've

done very well. Definitely worth the cost of two soul pearls. What time of day is it there?"

"Midafternoon I'd say, why?"

"I can't open the portal until the sun has set in your location. Is your position secure enough to wait eight hours?"

"I'm in no immediate danger. If you know where the artifact is, then eight hours more or less is irrelevant. I'll be ready when you are."

"Good." Fane severed the connection and grinned. At last, the final piece of the puzzle had fallen into place. Opening a portal to such a distant location would require considerable power. Luckily, she had plenty of Black Bile on hand.

If she had to use all of it, that would be a small enough price for ultimate victory.

CHAPTER 24

Joran brushed dirt from his tunic and held his blue light higher. The entry area of the underground workshop was roughly circular and had three doors leading out of it. None were labeled, so he assumed anyone coming here would already know where they were supposed to go.

Mia stood beside him, sword drawn and ready despite the lack of any visible threat. Guilt for what happened to Grub radiated off her in waves despite the dwarf's repeated assurances that it wasn't her fault. Samaritan was a sneaky bastard and bad things happened in battle. Mia knew all that, but it didn't seem to help any. Maybe once they got home and away from all the corruption, she'd feel better. He certainly hoped so.

"Which way?" Joran asked.

Bahesti looked from door to door before finally pointing to the center one. "Straight ahead, I believe."

"You believe?" Mia sounded as incredulous as he felt.

"I've never been inside one of the workshops. I accompanied my mistress here once, but wasn't allowed to enter. Wizards only, you know. Anyway, the whole facility isn't that big.

Searching the entire thing shouldn't take more than an hour at most."

"Sounds plenty long to me." Grub slurred his words, a side effect of the pain medication Joran had given him.

Stoneheart still did his best to prop his fellow dwarf up. He hadn't even made any nasty comments since the fight.

"Straight ahead is as good a place to start as any." Joran took a step and Mia immediately moved in front of him. "Ladies first, by all means."

She favored him with a slightly sheepish look. "Sorry. Feeling a little overprotective, you know."

"In that case, perhaps my golem should go first," Bahesti said.

Without waiting for a response, he pointed at the door and the golem clumped over and yanked it open. No magic lashed at it and no monsters roared out to attack. After the battle above, both of these results suited Joran perfectly well. No one wanted a fight; they just wanted to get home.

The group strode down a hall every bit as plain as the entry room. There weren't even sconces for torches. Since it was mostly wizards visiting, Joran figured they had no trouble supplying their own magic.

"Does this seem a little too easy to anyone else?" Mia asked.

"This isn't a vault or treasury," Bahesti said. "There would have been guards above, but once you were inside, no one wanted to worry about putting a foot wrong and getting a leg blown off. This place was constantly busy, filled with some of the most powerful wizards in the empire. Anyone stupid enough to try and sneak in to cause mischief would quickly come to regret their decision."

It reminded Joran of the imperial alchemy labs, heavily guarded on the outside but once you were inside, you had nothing to worry about. Or so he hoped. At this point he took nothing for granted.

They kept walking down undecorated halls and past

unmarked doors. The scent of chemicals, faint but still clear, filled the air. Joran didn't dare breathe too deeply, but the familiar odor of alchemy actually soothed him in a way clean, fresh air never could.

Bahesti didn't stop to look behind any of them. For someone that claimed he'd never been here before, he certainly acted sure of himself. Somehow Joran doubted he'd gotten a detailed description of the place from his mistress. Maybe he had a reason for not telling them the truth. As long as they reached the portal and made it home, he didn't care what secrets Bahesti kept.

At the end of the hall, they finally stopped in front of a black door marked with what Joran recognized as an overrune. Of course, he still had no idea what it meant, but at least he recognized it.

"The overrune marks this as the portal chamber," Bahesti said.

"Great. Are we waiting for anything in particular?" Joran asked. Now that they were so close, he wanted to get it over with.

"No. I suppose it seemed a sort of momentous accomplishment and I wanted to take a second to savor our success."

"While I appreciate the sentiment," Joran said. "I think we'd all just as soon get on our way."

Mia offered an emphatic nod.

"Of course." Bahesti put his hand on the door and pushed it inward.

Torches burst to life all around a chamber about twice the size of the one near Dwarfhome. In the center of the room, a bile pool about ten feet across shimmered in the light. Deeply carved overrunes surrounded it, but beyond that the chamber was empty.

"It's really small," Mia said.

Joran had been thinking the same thing. "The pool that

brought us here was at least three times bigger than this one. Are you certain it has enough power to get us back?"

"Of course. Remember, this pool is connected to the one in the colonies and both will be drained when it activates, completing the loop. And even if it wasn't, a pool of this size has power enough and then some to do whatever you need it to short of leveling a modest city."

"I assume we need to offer a complete soul to activate it," Joran said.

"Not from this end. A soul sacrifice will activate any pool's magic. It's a backup process put in place just in case a mage needed to get back here in a hurry and for whatever reason lacked the power to teleport. To activate this one, all you need to do is feed magical energy into the rune that matches the one on the door. That will activate the process and in about thirty seconds everything and everyone will be transported to the other end of the portal."

Joran nodded. Sounded simple enough. "Thank you for all your help. We wouldn't have survived without it."

"Keep your end of the bargain and I will consider myself well paid. And for the sake of the world, learn from my people's mistakes. Stop the dragon from waking. I can't imagine what it might do if someone disturbed it again."

"We'll do our best. Mia?"

Joran and the dwarves moved deeper into the bile chamber.

Mia drew her sword and asked, "How do you want me to do this?"

Bahesti touched his neck. "Take my head. One clean blow will do it. And thank you for the mercy. Heaven knows I don't deserve it."

She raised the mithril sword. "I've never killed an ally before. It feels wrong."

Bahesti's face crinkled into an expression Joran didn't recognize. "If you knew half the things I've done in my long life, you'd have no compunction about killing me. Rest assured, I both deserve and desire death."

"If you say so." Mia drew back and swung.

The edge of her sword cut Bahesti's head off as easily as it seemed to cut everything else. His iron head hit the floor with a loud clang. His body stood where it was, still as the statue it now was. The golem stood just as still as Bahesti. Without its master it seemed to have no will of its own.

Joran reached out, took Mia's hand, and drew her into the chamber before closing the door and blocking out the sight of their dead comrade. "You gave him what he wanted. Take comfort in that. Hopefully he's found some sort of peace in whatever afterlife awaits him."

Grub snorted. "You likely freed his soul for a one-way trip to Hell."

Stoneheart smacked him on the back of the head. "Even if you're right, that's not the sort of thing you should say to Lady Mia right now."

"It's okay, Stoneheart. I don't harbor any illusions about the people of this land. He just didn't seem like such a bad guy."

"Seeing everything you've ever known reduced to blackened earth and corruption is apt to change your thinking." Joran quickly found the appropriate rune. "Grub, are you up to channeling the ether, or do you want me to do it?"

"My brain feels like mush after that stuff you gave me for the pain. You'd best do it."

Joran nodded. "Mia, would you help me?"

He appreciated that she didn't say there was nothing she could do and instead came to join him beside the rune. He put his hand on the hilt of her sword and switched his vision to the ether. With an effort of will he sent energy flowing into the rune. The power moved easily, easier than it ever had and he suspected the sword had a great deal to do with that.

When the whole rune had begun to glow and spread to the mark beside it, Joran ended the spell.

One by one the runes burst to life until the full circle glowed. A blinding flash filled the chamber and for an instant Joran felt like he was being torn apart.

And then it ended and he found himself in a natural cavern. Everyone had made the journey without issue. In the center of the chamber sat a now-empty bile pool. Joran shifted his vision and found the ether free of corruption. While he had no idea if they were actually in the Tiberian Empire, he was confident that they were no longer in the Black Iron Empire.

Joran conjured a white light and smiled at how good it felt to wield the pure ether. A cave at the back of the cavern provided the only exit, so the weary group headed for it. The smooth floor made for easy walking and soon enough a light appeared at the end of the tunnel, allowing Joran to end his spell. With the light came a breeze that smelled of rain and wet grass.

He doubted he'd ever smelled anything so wonderful.

"We're south of the capital for sure," Mia said. "That breeze is too warm."

"Not warm enough for Stello Province," he said. "What do you think, somewhere in between?"

Mia nodded. "About halfway I'd guess. Holden Province maybe. At least I hope so. That's always been the least restive. I don't think I ever heard Alexandra complain about it and she complained about most of them at least once."

They emerged from the tunnel and a patchwork of farms spread out below them. They'd ended up on the side of a hill overlooking a farming community. How had the locals not noticed the tunnel and bile pool below?

He looked back in time to watch an illusion shimmer into place over the cave entrance. When it finished you couldn't even tell that a cave had ever been there. That explained one mystery at least.

"Let's see if we can convince a farmer to give us a ride to the nearest garrison. I need to get a message to the palace as soon as possible."

———

Alexandra lay on her bed and stared up at the ceiling. She'd been trying to nap for a while with no success. After seeing the dragon ship off and reporting to her father, all she wanted to do was sleep, but it continued to elude her. At least her body was resting even if her mind couldn't.

She yawned and rolled over on the soft mattress. Hopefully between the White Knights and the Fourth Legion, the wizard and his monsters would be dealt with quickly. The empire had enough problems without lunatics and bile zombies running around causing chaos.

A faint knock from outside reached her. She squeezed her eyes shut. Please don't let it be another problem.

Murmured voices were followed by the door closing and another knock, louder this time, on her bedroom door.

A very unladylike curse slipped out. "I said I didn't want to be disturbed."

"An important message has arrived for you, Majesty," Marsa said. "I really think you need to see it."

Well, she couldn't sleep anyway. Alexandra rolled out of bed and strode over to the door. The servant stood, head bowed, a three-inch-long, rolled-up scroll held out in her hands. She snatched it out of the servant's hand and read the outside.

It said, "Princess Alexandra."

Who would write to her directly and in such an informal manner? There weren't many nobles of such high rank that would dare.

Frowning, she pulled off the band holding it closed and started reading.

Alexandra,

We have returned safely after a difficult journey. I hope to be on the way to Tiber at first light. There is much I need to tell you.

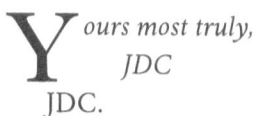

Yours most truly,
JDC

JDC.

Tears filled her eyes. Joran was back. Alexandra knew in her heart that he'd survived even if no one else believed her. And she was right. He was back and on his way home.

She looked up and found Marsa staring at her with shining eyes. "You were right, Majesty. Lord Den Cade is okay."

"How did you know?" Alexandra asked.

"I recognized his handwriting on the scroll. I've carried many messages for him since he arrived. The girls will be so pleased. Will you tell your father?"

"I don't think so, not until he arrives. Let it be a pleasant surprise. We should do something nice for him when he gets home. Where did the scroll come from?"

"Garrison Fort Three in Holden Province. How do you suppose he ended up there of all places?"

Alexandra hadn't the slightest idea. No doubt Joran would tell them himself when he arrived. At least he'd ended up in the safest province and not too far away either. If they made good time, he should reach Tiber in about two weeks.

A shiver ran through her. She could hardly wait to see him.

CHAPTER 25

Much as he hated waiting, Samaritan found the spot Gomo had chosen quite peaceful. Or at least as peaceful as any place in this miserable wasteland could be. The sun had set hours ago and true darkness covered the land. A darkness far deeper than anything he'd ever experienced anywhere else. The cloud cover kept the moonlight blocked out and only the modest hellfire Gomo had summoned allowed him to see his hand in front of his face.

"How long are we going to wait here?" Overmage asked.

The metal man had returned, without his golem, an hour after Samaritan reached the clearing. A secret part of him had hoped the obnoxious man had been killed, but as with most of his hopes, Samaritan was doomed to disappointment.

"Is there somewhere you need to be?" Samaritan asked. "You're not tied down. Feel free to leave anytime."

Overmage growled, a tinny little rasp in the back of his throat. "There are other options for getting where we need to go. Other bile portals. This archbishop that you hold so much faith in might not even be powerful enough to open a portal this far away."

"You might be right, though she seemed confident of success. In truth, I've seen her open small portals before, so I know she can do it." Samaritan shrugged. "Either way, for now at least, I'm too tired to set out for a different island. If the archbishop hasn't made contact by morning, we'll discuss other options."

Overmage dropped to the dirt like a petulant child, drawing a chuckle from Gomo. The demon had been quiet for hours and Samaritan had begun to wonder if something was wrong with him, besides the missing arm.

He pushed the question aside when a familiar charge ran through the amulet. Samaritan closed his eyes and drew ether through the metal. "Archbishop?"

Were you expecting someone else? I've made the necessary preparations to bring you here. But I will need your help. That was something he never imagined her saying. *All you need to do is pour as much ether as you can into the amulet and then pull it back out, purifying the area so the corruption doesn't interfere with the portal. I'll handle the rest.*

"How long should I do it?" he asked.

Until the portal forms. Once it does, don't dawdle. As best I can tell, you're on the far side of the world; even I can't maintain a portal of that distance for long.

Yet another admission he never imagined her making.

Taking a steadying breath, Samaritan pulled corrupt ether into the amulet and pushed pure ether out. The first few times he did this, the energy field around him looked no different, but after half a minute, the immediate area started to clear.

The sight of his efforts bearing fruit drove Samaritan on. After a full minute, the area around him looked nearly as pure as back home.

The archbishop must have sensed it as well. Ether crackled around the amulet, singeing his skin through his tunic. Slowly, a silver circle formed. At first only big enough for an arm to pass through. It expanded inch by inch until Gomo could pass through without ducking.

Exhaustion started to take its toll and Samaritan doubted he could continue purifying the ether for much longer.

Luckily her voice appeared in his head. *That's the best I can do. It's now or never.*

Samaritan didn't need to be told twice.

He dove through, landing on a hard, stone floor covered in black tile. A moment later Gomo strode through and moved to the right.

Samaritan's eyes widened and he rolled left a moment before Overmage crashed to the floor beside him.

The portal vanished, leaving nothing but floating crimson lights to see by.

The archbishop's perfect face appeared above him. "I felt certain you were dead. What a nice surprise to find I was mistaken. Though you did fail to mention you planned to bring this rabble with you."

"Mind your tongue, woman, lest I rip it out." Gomo took a step toward the archbishop.

She turned to look at him and Gomo froze. Chains of sizzling energy appeared around his neck, waist, and arms. A subtle gesture of her right hand and the chains dragged Gomo to the floor.

"I will not be threatened by a forgeling in my own casting chamber." Gomo howled in pain as more energy shot through the chains. "I don't know which hell spat you out, though from the look of you I'd guess you were one of Abaddon's creations, but if you want to see that miserable pit again, you'd best mind your manners. Should you do otherwise, I'll bind your essence to a gem and bury you in the heart of a glacier. Do we understand each other?"

"Yes!" The word came out as a tortured scream. "My most

humble apologies for my rudeness. I failed to recognize your true power. I promise to serve you to the best of my ability."

"That's better." The chains vanished. "What are you called?"

"He said his name is Gomo," Samaritan offered.

The archbishop laughed. "The absolute arrogance of a mere forgeling daring to take the name, even in part, of one of the nine. Remarkable. What do you suppose The Torturer would do should he find out?"

"I prefer not to think about it," Gomo said. "May I stand, Mistress?"

"By all means." She shifted her attention to Overmage, who had already regained his feet. "And this?"

"You may call me Overmage. I was once one of the rulers of the Black Iron Empire. When the dragon of corruption attacked, all the others were destroyed and I ended up transformed into what you see before you."

"The dragon did this to you and yet you still wish to wake it again. Why?"

"My reasons are my own. Let it be sufficient that we both desire the same thing. I will do everything in my power to help you claim the locating device. I swear on my honor as an overmage."

She glanced at Samaritan who shrugged. "He's been of considerable help since we met. Of course, if you already know where to find the artifact, I don't know how much more help he can be."

"As long as he causes me no difficulties, I'm content to let him tag along on the off chance some of his knowledge might come in handy." The archbishop faced Samaritan full on and he was struck once more by how someone so beautiful could also be so cold and soulless. "You and I need to have a long talk. You two will remain here. When it's time to collect the artifact, I'll return to transport us there."

Neither Gomo nor Overmage argued and a moment later

Samaritan found himself following the archbishop through the dark halls of her citadel. Wherever they were going, he hoped it wasn't far and that a comfortable chair awaited him. He had seldom been as tired as he felt right now.

His wish came true when less than a minute later they ducked into a dining room free of the corruption that filled her citadel nearly as thickly as it did the Black Iron Empire. A table big enough to seat twenty but set for only one filled the center of the room. A plate loaded with meat, vegetables, and bread awaited his attention. A glass of pure, clear water might have been the second most beautiful sight he'd ever seen in his life.

"Eat and rest," she said. "I can wait until you're finished."

Samaritan didn't need to be told twice. He sat in front of the plate and dug in to the most delicious meal he'd ever tasted. Halfway through he looked up. "I didn't know you had a room like this."

"I keep it for those occasions when I entertain living guests. It gets very little use."

He didn't doubt that in the least. The thought of the archbishop holding a dinner party struck him as the most absurd idea he'd ever encountered.

When he finished the last of the incredibly tender beef she asked, "What happened, Samaritan? Tell me everything."

He took a breath and did so, starting with his shock at finding a portal where he expected to find a giant beast, through his meetings with Overmage and Gomo, and ending with the battle for the second bile portal.

When he'd told her everything he added, "If the dragon could do that to the Black Iron Empire, think what it will do to the Tiberian Empire. I'll wake it and say Emperor Tiberius sent me to make a slave of it or something equally insulting. If this thing's as ill-tempered as it sounds, that should be enough to rouse its wrath. Picturing Tiber reduced to black iron and rubble fills my heart with joy."

"Do you picture yourself surviving this encounter?"

"No, and I don't care. As long as the empire dies, my life is a small price. One I'd gladly pay a hundred times over if I had to. You haven't changed your mind about waking it, have you?"

The archbishop pursed ruby-red lips. "No, waking it is still the best way to get what I want. However, if it rampages across this continent the way it did the other, my citadel may be damaged and that wouldn't suit me at all. I've expended a great deal of time and magic making this place over to my liking. Perhaps it won't wake at all when we approach. If so, that might suit me just as well. Either way, I still wish to see it with my own eyes."

Samaritan nodded but didn't like the sound of her new ambivalence. Whether she liked it or not, he would find a way to wake the dragon. He yawned, then said, "Is there any way I can get a brief nap before we go?"

"Certainly. I need to make preparations for opening a second portal, not to mention it's still daytime on this side of the world. Rest, sleep if you can. I'll return to get you when it's time to leave. You'll find no more comfortable room in the citadel. A bed, I fear, is too much to hope for."

"I spend more time sleeping on the ground than I do in a bed anyway. Your floor will suit me fine."

She stood. "Then rest well. From the sounds of it, you've earned the break."

When she'd closed the door behind her, Samaritan curled up on the floor and fell into a deep sleep. As soon as he did, he dreamed of black flames and red slaughter as Tiber suffered under the dragon's rage. Had anyone been in the room with him, they'd have wondered at the little smile that creased his lips.

CHAPTER 26

Samaritan stepped through a much larger and more stable portal and appeared in a field surrounded by forest. A normal field with actual grass and living trees made of wood instead of black iron. Overhead the moon shone down from a cloudless sky. Being back in something approaching the normal world felt amazing. The only thing missing was a fortress.

"Where are we?" he asked when the archbishop joined them and closed the portal.

"Near the eastern ocean. Something about the artifact prevents magical transportation so we need to walk a mile or so to get there. It's actually an interesting effect and if it weren't such a nuisance, I'd like to study it closer. As it is, I can easily create something similar so why waste the time?"

"What are we waiting for now?" Overmage asked. "I can sense the artifact from here. Let's go."

Gomo, at least, had the good sense to remain silent. No doubt the archbishop's earlier display of power had a great deal to do with his lack of comment.

"Your pet statue like to talk."

Samaritan shook his head. "Overmage isn't anything of mine. Had I the power to get him to shut up, I'd have used it long before now."

Overmage glared at them and stomped off through the forest.

"Sensitive as well. His soul might be worth studying when this is over." The archbishop set out behind Overmage.

The walk took only minutes and soon they were crossing the drawbridge of a standard church fortress. Samaritan had seen plenty of them during his time as a White Knight. This one might be a little bigger than usual, but that was the only thing interesting about it.

They crossed the yard and he made of point of ignoring the bloodstains in the sand and other signs of battle. The White Knights weren't his allies anymore and he didn't care if they were torn apart by some undead horror.

Inside, they wove a path through the halls until they reached the room that led to the basement. An overseer stood just inside the door. It bowed to the archbishop. "No change, Mistress. The humans have made no attempt to escape and the flow of corruption remains the same."

"Exactly as expected," the archbishop said. "Let's go ahead and kill the humans then Samaritan can collect the artifact for us."

The overseer pulled a vial out of its robe. A dark mist swirled beyond the glass. "I have Dread Spores. Combined with a wind spell, it should be enough to handle them."

"Ha!" Overmage stomped toward the doorway. "Don't waste your magic. I'll deal with them myself. Follow in a moment, human."

"Can't you bring it up yourself?" Samaritan asked.

Overmage paused and looked back. "No. The magic is designed to allow only a living human to touch it."

That seemed tremendously unlikely, but Samaritan

shrugged. He'd do whatever he had to in order to find the dragon. "I'll join you in five minutes."

"Make it two. They're only humans."

The metal man clanked down the steps out of sight.

"I can sense the corruption filling that thing," the overseer said. "How can it approach when we can't?"

The archbishop shook her head. "It's essentially a construct, maybe that has something to do with it."

"The ether can't touch any of the people transformed into black iron," Gomo said. "Spells don't affect them and they in turn can't cast spells. That likely has more to do with it than anything."

"What a horrendous curse to place on a wizard." Archbishop shuddered as if contemplating such a fate herself. "This dragon truly is evil."

The crash of steel on iron ended the conversation. Screams from dying men soon followed.

Samaritan waited until silence fell then started down the steps. He felt nothing out of the ordinary as he made his way down to the basement. When he imagined the final stage of his revenge, he always thought it would bring more emotions. Instead, he felt nothing but grim determination to see it done. Once he completed his mission, death would be welcome.

At the bottom of the stairs, Samaritan stepped over the crushed body of a White Knight. He didn't look too closely, but even a glance made it clear he was a young man, probably not more than six months out of training.

The carnage continued, forcing him to pick his way around broken and dismembered bodies. The pristine white cloaks looked completely out of place amidst the slaughter.

When he finally reached Overmage, he found the metal man standing beside an inky black orb resting on a pedestal of equally dark metal. Blood dripped from his hands and spattered his body. A disgusting sight for sure.

"Go on," Overmage said.

Samaritan reached out. The air around the orb felt cold, colder than anything he'd ever experienced before. Even the mountains near Dwarfhome seemed warm by comparison. At least it didn't hurt.

Finally he placed a hand on the orb.

The world went dark and it felt like he was rushing through space even though he knew it had to be an illusion. When the sensation stopped, he found himself floating in the dark, but not alone. A figure faced him. A man in black, high-collared robes. His skin was a dark-bronze color, darker than Samaritan's but not as dark as the people of the lands just north of Stello Province.

But what really caught his attention were the man's eyes. They glowed the color of polished gold.

"You seek the dragon," the man said. "You've seen what it did to my homeland and you wish to see the same thing done to yours. Such powerful hate."

"Who are you?" Samaritan asked. "Some sort of guide bound to the orb?"

"Hardly. My name is Khashair and I was one of the over-mages that ruled the Black Iron Empire."

"Were you a friend of the one that brought me here?"

Khashair laughed. "I had no friends and if I did, a citadel defense automaton certainly wouldn't have been one of them. I made the automaton and left a logic program in its head that would prompt it to think it was me and do anything possible to bring someone here. You see, while my spirit remains strong, I need a new host if I'm to return to life. Which brings us to you."

"Are you going to wake the dragon?" Samaritan considered that highly unlikely, but needed to ask.

"Are you mad? The beast is nothing but death and destruction. I want to rule a new empire not see the rest of the world reduced to the same sorry state as my former home. Not what you wanted to hear, I take it?"

"In that case I can't serve as your host. I have my own mission to complete."

Khashair shook his head. "I don't require your permission. Your body is mine. I simply haven't taken full possession yet. I wanted to speak with you first, see what sort of man you were. It doesn't matter to me, you understand, but I haven't spoken to anyone in centuries."

"Why didn't you just take one of the knights?"

"Their souls weren't corrupt enough to be of any use. The evil you've done mirrors my own. The darkness of our souls align. I see you met your soulmate and lost her. A great tragedy. But rejoice, your soul will soon be bound to mine. A forced binding isn't nearly as powerful as the real thing, but it is sufficient to allow me to control your body."

"What happens to me?"

"Do you care?" Khashair asked. "You live on the edge of killing yourself every day. I can see it plainly. Forcing yourself to face each day takes every ounce of willpower you can muster. That's a horrid way to live. Don't resist me and you'll never have to face that decision again. You can simply ride along and enjoy the show. I give you my word that I will destroy the church you hate so much."

Samaritan stared at the figure in black. No more decisions, or plotting, or revenge sounded like a dream come true. And he sensed that Khashair meant what he said about destroying the church, though he doubted he'd do it for Samaritan's sake. More likely he wanted to eliminate a potential competitor for power.

Not that Samaritan cared. As long as the ones responsible for her death were made to pay, that was enough.

"Agreed. Do what you must. I will offer no resistance."

Khashair flashed perfect white teeth then his eyes glowed

brighter. Soon Samaritan could see nothing else. Not long after that he felt nothing else.

———

"What's taking so long?" Fane snarled and stalked back and forth just out of range of the destructive effect. "He's been down there for half an hour. All he had to do was go down, grab the orb, and bring it up. How hard is that?"

"Maybe he's dead," her overseer said. "I can't tell through all the corruption still swirling around."

Fane hated to admit it, but she couldn't either. It would be a cruel irony if she expended so much effort to bring Samaritan here only to have him fail at the end. Even worse, it would put her back right where she began, with no way to reach the artifact.

She turned to start another pass when the corruption vanished. It wasn't subtle either. She blinked and it was gone. A moment later, footsteps sounded on the stairs.

Finally.

Samaritan emerged from the basement empty-handed with the obnoxious statue behind him. Neither of them held a black orb.

She bared her fangs. "Where is the artifact?"

Samaritan reached into his pocket and pulled out a black orb perhaps six inches in diameter. "It has served its purpose and is now powerless."

Fane frowned. His voice had changed. Not the tone but the accent. It was subtle, but definitely different.

"Do you know where to find the dragon?" she asked.

"I do, but I have no intention of waking the beast. Better for the world if it sleeps forever. My new empire will not be destroyed like the last one."

That sealed it. "Who are you and what have you done with

Samaritan? The former White Knight and I had an arrangement and I mean to see it carried out."

"Our souls are bonded, but I am dominant. My name is Khashair and I am the last overmage. I have seen you in Samaritan's memories and acknowledge your strength. I offer you this chance to serve at my right hand as the new empire's second overmage."

Fane straightened. Of all the arrogance. "I acknowledge only one person as my superior and that certainly isn't you. Tell me where to find the dragon and we can part ways peacefully."

"The dragon will not wake while it is within my power to prevent it. And if you will not submit, then you will die."

She didn't even see the spell form before she found herself flying across the room to slam into the far wall.

Fane's undead body didn't so much as bruise, but the power behind that blast shook her to the core.

With a psychic command she sent her overseer charging toward Khashair.

It managed to cover half the distance before threads of corrupt ether pierced it and ripped it apart.

It appeared to be the same effect that protected the artifact.

She had no hope of winning this fight. Not now.

Fane became one with the ether and fled.

Fled for now, but only for now. She would get her revenge for this humiliation and when she did, Khashair and Samaritan both would pay.

EPILOGUE

O n a beautiful late winter day, the thin layer of snow covering everything glittering in the sun, Joran and his group arrived in sight of Tiber. Instead of riding horses, they'd secured transport in the back of a military supply wagon. That made the trip more comfortable for everyone, but especially the dwarves. Only the Dwarfhome legion kept riding gear sized for dwarves and Joran seriously doubted Grub would have done well one handed even if they had the right gear.

The wagon also came with a full century acting as escort. It seemed excessive since they were traveling through the imperial heartland, but the garrison commander insisted that nothing would happen to the Iron Princess's fiancé on his watch. He said this with the grim tone of a man that understood exactly what would happen to his career should something happen to Joran on his watch.

In truth, Joran didn't actually mind the escort. After everything they'd been through, all he wanted was to rest and let the soldiers handle everything. He occupied himself by reading the journal he'd brought back from the Black Iron Empire a second time.

Most of it detailed the journey to the dragon's resting place and the many tribes the overmages slaughtered along the way. The names given meant little to Joran, but he did recognize some of the landmarks. He felt confident that when he sat down in front of a map of the empire, he'd be able to puzzle out the route. Then it was simply a matter of retracing their steps and setting up a garrison to prevent anyone else from reaching the beast.

He frowned and closed his eyes. All his plans assumed that the dragon still slept in the same place. Given that humans had found it once, it might have chosen to relocate. On the one hand, that would make it incredibly hard to find it and build a fortress, but on the other, it would be equally hard for Samaritan or anyone else to find the dragon, which would be no bad thing.

"Why is everything so complicated?" Joran muttered.

"If our problems were easy to solve, anyone could do it," Mia said. She rested shoulder-to-shoulder beside him, her mithril sword lying across her lap.

"That wouldn't be so bad. I could go back to the lab and resume my studies without anyone trying to kill me on a regular basis."

"What about me?" Mia asked.

"I've been debating that very thing. Assuming things ever calm down enough that we can enjoy something like a normal life, I thought you might enjoy teaching a class on swordsmanship. There's an open area not far from my lab on campus that would be perfect and well within range of our link."

"I don't know anything about teaching." Mia sounded intrigued despite herself.

"You'd be a natural."

"Approaching the gates, Lord Den Cade," Stoneheart said from his perch on the driver's bench.

"Excellent, take us right to the palace. There shouldn't be any trouble until we reach Third Circle."

In fact, traveling with a full century of legionnaires as a personal guard served to convince even the guards at Third Circle's gate to open up with a minimum of fuss. Sooner than you might have expected the wagon rattled to a stop in front of the side door that led right to Alexandra's suite. The guards on duty snapped to attention when they saw Joran stand up in the back.

Everyone jumped down from the wagon, Joran wincing at his stiff back. A quick stretch worked the kinks out and he walked over to the unit commander.

"Many thanks for the escort, Centurion." Joran shook the slightly flummoxed man's hand. "Head to the barracks and tell them I sent you. They'll get you a hot meal and find you a place to sleep for the night. Please extend my thanks to the garrison commander when you get back."

"Aye, Lord Den Cade. I'll do that, sir."

He released the man with a final pat on the shoulder and smiled as he put as much distance as quickly as decorum would allow between himself and this den of nobility. Sensible man. They'd need as many of those as they could find if things went as badly as Joran feared they might.

Joran led the way to the door at a still-weary trudge. "Good day, gentlemen. If you'd be so kind as to let us in, I'm eager for a hot meal and a bath."

"We wouldn't dare keep you, my lord," the right-hand guard said, already reaching for the door. "Her Majesty informed every guard at every entrance that if you were delayed by even a breath, the men on duty would find themselves rotated out to Stello Province within the week. I believe she meant it."

Joran grinned. "I suspect she did too. Rest assured, Alexandra will hear no word of complaint from me."

"The One God bless you, my lord."

"So say we all." Joran made the circle despite feeling like a hypocrite.

The ragged quartet made the familiar walk to Alexandra's suite. His knuckle had barely touched the door when it opened and Marsa, smiling, hugged him. "We were all so worried, Lord Den Cade. But Her Majesty never doubted you were still alive."

"I appreciate Alexandra's faith in me. Is she here?"

The bedroom door opened and Alexandra stood there staring at him. Joran doubted she'd ever looked more beautiful. She wore a simple gown of blue and silver that left her shoulders bare. Her dark hair had grown longer and framed her perfect face.

"I'm back," he said.

Alexandra sprinted across the waiting room and leapt into his arms.

Joran spun her around and held her tight, breathing deep the scent of her rose perfume. In the back of his mind Mia's pleasure held a softer note than her usual lustful thoughts.

When he finally set her down Alexandra said, "Took you long enough to get home."

"Considering we traveled halfway around the world, I thought we made pretty good time." Despite his pleasure at the reunion, Joran forced himself to get to business. "Much as I'd like to spend the rest of the day with you, I need to get to the lab and brew a cure all for Grub. The good dwarf lost a hand in battle with our enemies."

The mask of the Iron Princess slipped back in place. "Samaritan?"

"Escaped, again. We have a great deal to discuss. Perhaps tonight over dinner with your father and brother."

"Good idea. I'll make the arrangements. Then after dinner, you and I will have a… private discussion."

Joran's smile returned. He would certainly look forward to that and from the tingle in the back of his mind, so would Mia.

AUTHOR NOTE

Hello everyone,

By some miracle Joran and his companions made it home in one piece, or mostly one piece in Grub's case. Unfortunately for everyone, Samaritan made it back as well. Now it's a rush to the final confrontation. Will the empire survive or will Samaritan finally get his long desired revenge?

I hope you'll join me next time when Joran, Mia, and Alexandra's adventure comes to its exciting conclusion in Overmage.

You can find links to all my books on my website, www.jamesewisher.com

Thanks for reading and I'll see you next time.

James

ALSO BY JAMES E WISHER

The Slave War

The Sunken Tower

The Dragon Empress

The Dragonspire Chronicles Omnibus Vol. 1

The Dragonspire Chronicles Omnibus Vol. 2

The Complete Dragonspire Chronicles Omnibus

Soul Force Saga

Disciples of the Horned One Trilogy:

Darkness Rising

Raging Sea and Trembling Earth

Harvest of Souls

Disciples of the Horned One Omnibus

Chains of the Fallen Arc:

Dreaming in the Dark

On Blackened Wings

Chains of the Fallen Omnibus

The Complete Soul Force Saga Omnibus

The Aegis of Merlin:

The Impossible Wizard

The Awakening

The Chimera Jar

The Raven's Shadow

Escape From the Dragon Czar

Wrath of the Dragon Czar

The Four Nations Tournament

Death Incarnate

Atlantis Rising

Rise of the Demon Lords

The Pale Princess

Aegis of Merlin Omnibus Vol 1.

Aegis of Merlin Omnibus Vol 2.

The Complete Aegis of Merlin Omnibus

Other Fantasy Novels:

The Squire

Death and Honor Omnibus

The Rogue Star Series:

Children of Darkness

Children of the Void

Children of Junk

Rogue Star Omnibus Vol. 1

Children of the Black Ship

ABOUT THE AUTHOR

James E. Wisher is a writer of science fiction and fantasy novels. He's been writing since high school and reading everything he could get his hands on for as long as he can remember.

To learn more:
www.jamesewisher.com
james@jamesewisher.com